DON'T EVEN THINK IT

*If a girl loses her temper does it
have to become a thing?*

Linda Dawe

ACKNOWLEDGMENTS

My thanks go to colleague and mentor Phil Parker for pointing out that the original screenplay 'had no third act', to readers Marilyn Griffin, Ruth Worboys, Katy Newell-Jones and Wally Landsberg who all added to the mix, and to Sara-Jane Reeves for her professional proof-reading services.

A special mention goes to Watkin's bookshop in Cecil Court, London, where I first picked up a copy of Dion Fortune's *Psychic Self Defense* and read the line: 'I myself once had an exceedingly nasty experience in which I formulated a werewolf accidentally.'

Don't Even Think It is a classic rom-com with a horror twist proving that expressing your anger can have dangerous outcomes not of this world.

Philip Parker, *The Art & Science of Screenwriting*

CONTENTS

Prologue

Little Red

I was never quite myself again
after that incident at Granny's.
He gulped me down in one
like a quail's egg canapé:
bathing in lupine gastric juice
does something to a girl.

I stepped out of his reeking carcass
newborn;
developed a taste for raw meat,
felt restless each full moon,
and when my monthlies came around
I howled
for something far more powerful
than paracetamol.

Now I am wolf and woman
at home in neither world:
the mundane human realm, or
the deep forests of the beast.
Pity me if you must,
but keep a safe distance.

Chapter 1

Tibet

Five o'clock on a misty morning is no time to be stuck halfway up the Brecon Beacons without a Portaloo. (All this happened a while ago before the Brecon Beacons was romantically renamed Bannau Brycheiniog, or the Peaks of Brychan's Kingdom.) So 5 a.m. halfway up, without a Portaloo. And Cassandra Green wished they could just get on with it. But the sun wasn't going to rise any faster for wishing.

The gravel road behind her was lined with production vehicles: a coach for the supporting artistes and the dressers, a disgusting old white van (Grips or Sparks) three or four hatchbacks (Gaffer, Best Boy and sound crew) and the Director's little red number. Below that was the star's Winnebago. The caterers' wagon was parked further down the hillside, serving up the traditional greasy location breakfast from 4 a.m. and buckets of industrial strength tea and coffee. You needed scalding hot tea to keep out the cold. And the Portaloos still hadn't arrived. Try not to think about it.

The FX guy brushed past Cass, swirling knee-deep dry ice. Even the ground mist was not real. He puffed some more around the entrance to a Tibetan yurt perched on the Welsh hillside, as they waited for sunrise. Cass wasn't sure if it was technically a 'yurt' or not, but she liked the word. She pulled her favourite old filming hat further down on her head and stuck her hands into the pockets of her duvet coat for a moment's warmth. Layers of thermal underwear and a woolly fisherman's jersey turned her into a walking barrel, but what of it? At five in the morning she didn't give a damn about how she looked.

The Director squinted at the horizon, checked his watch and gave her the nod.

'Quiet please, going for a take,' said Cass. The Director of Photography took this as his cue to vanish into the bushes for another quick slash. It's OK for him, Cass thought bitterly. God, this is no life for a girl. She'd begun thinking that more and more lately. Production Assistant was OK when you were in your early twenties, but by now she should have some producer credits to her name.

'And – cue Greta!'

Alexandra David-Kneel, 1920s French explorer opened the flap of the yurt and stepped out into the pale light of a new dawn over Tibet. Alexandra, the female lead played by soap star Greta Stratton, was dressed in fake suede Tibetan travelling clothes and leather boots. Greta had refused to wear the Tibetan hat as it would have spoiled her hair and frankly looked ridiculous. The designer had caved on that point, so no silly hats now or ever. The figure of a Shaman followed Greta chanting and drumming on a little hand drum.

The Brecon Beacons wasn't a bad choice of location. It

could pass for Tibet. If you didn't know what Tibet looked like. The intrepid woman explorer and Shaman greeted the rising sun, behind them lurked the dark robed figure of a Zen monk – a figure of evil. According to the screenplay this monk was a *tulpa* drawing the life-force out of Alexandra, who had dreamed him up as an experiment in thought projection. Post-production CGI would add in a truly terrifying monk later. For the moment it was a bloke in a mackintosh, yawning and scratching his backside.

The Shaman only had two lines to deliver: 'Madam, your thoughts alone created something beyond your control, be careful…be careful... oh, bugger, bollocks, bugger, can we go again?'

'Keep going,' the Director's voice buzzed in Cass's earpiece.

'We're rolling, going for another take,' she announced. The Makeup Girl, young and eager, rushed into shot to tidy up her lady's hair. Greta, recently come out of the soaps, with a voice like sandpaper, was still quite a catch. Low budget indie horror films don't usually strike it so lucky.

'Still rolling!' Cass shouted, and the Makeup Girl ducked out of shot. The actors slipped back into the yurt. The sun continued to rise. The actors emerged, the Shaman began conjuring the spectral figure of the Zen monk to disappear.

'And we've cut!' At least the Director was pleased. He was only a year older than Cass and had previously made a couple of teen comedies. They were crap.

'Checking the gate,' Cass called.

A pale red sun was rising over the hills, and with any luck

that was a wrap. Noise levels began rising, as the crew and cast relaxed. All around were the supporting artistes dressed as Sherpas, or something ethnic. They'd been bussed out from Cardiff in the early hours and could turn nasty if they were left out in the cold for too long.

Greta whinged that she was freezing and Mac came running to swathe her in a blanket. Mac, the lady dresser, pushing sixty, wheezed as they trudged back to the star's Winnebago. Once Mac had been 'a trained actress' herself but dressing paid more.

From the corner of her eye Cass saw Animal strutting over. Why it is every crew has to have an Animal on it? Is it union rules? This one was even called 'Animal'. Maybe it was something to do with the wild, unkempt hair. Or jeans slung too low around the incipient beer gut, revealing bum cleavage at every bend. All men are Animals, but at least some have evolved to buy jeans that fit. If he put an arm around her waist again, she'd hit him over the head with her production book.

'Coming to the party tonight, Flash?' Animal said.

'No, I'm not,' Cass snapped. 'No one's going to hang around this godforsaken place any longer than –'

'No good for focus,' the Focus Puller announced. Cass winced.

'Can we go for it again?' the Director asked her.

'Not unless you can get the sun to rise again. That was fuckin' obvious, wasn't it?'

The Director swore and said that he only hoped the production budget could stand it, because there goes our standby day, and that shitty bloody hotel would have to put the whole unit up for one more night, and Cass better get on to it right away, because he was going off to have a nervous breakdown with his partner, the Producer.

'OK folks, that's a wrap,' said Cass. 'We'll book you in for one more overnight and the call will be 4 a.m. tomorrow morning. Supporting artistes, back on the coach please.' Jimbo, the boys' dresser, began shepherding the extras towards their transport, as Cass reached for her phone to call the hotel.

It's amazing how quickly a location can clear – no sooner were the words 'that's a wrap' out of her mouth than the Director was off, Sparks, Grips, Props and FX were shooting away down the gravel track, the Winnebago de-camped with the star and her wardrobe; leaving Cass, Mac, Jimbo and the little Makeup Girl to push a coachload of supporting artistes out of the mud.

'Where are all the big strong men when you need them?' said Jimbo. 'Three wee lassies and a poofta left to push a fifty-seater off a mountain.'

'Shut up and push,' said Mac, 'this isn't doing my back any good.'

Cass kept her mouth closed. She didn't want to eat Welsh hillside as the wheels splattered mud into her face. The coach driver assured them it only needed one more big push. Then he assured them that it would work if the coach was empty, so all the supporting artistes disembarked and stood around looking useless. They weren't insured to push heavy vehicles.

'No good,' said the driver, after a two more attempts at

rocking the coach free had failed. 'I'll have to phone for a tow out and minibus. The extras can wait on the coach till the minibus gets here.'

'Right,' said Cass, 'I'll call a taxi to pick us up down in the car park.'

*

'Coming to the party then?' asked Jimbo, as they trekked down the hillside. Jimbo was a stick-thin Scot of indeterminate age, with suede hair and a single earring.

'I suppose so, as we're stuck here,' said Cass, 'though I'd rather pull out my own toenails than spend another night fending off Animal.'

'You know why they call him Animal?' said the little Makeup Girl, linking her arm through Cass's.

'No? Why?' asked Jimbo.

'Not talking to you!'

'Sorry!' said Jimbo, dropping back with Mac.

'One of the Sparks shares a room with him over the pub,' said the Makeup Girl. 'They won't stay in the unit hotel 'cos it's too pricey. And it's too far to do a flier. He was telling us about Animal. They went out for a drink and he pulled this old bird – you know: really done up, but well in her thirties – and took her up to the room. When this other bloke, Mick, went up later, there was just Animal left. The sink was full of blood. She'd come-on, you know. And Mick goes "That's disgusting", but Animal took the hand towel and soaked it all up and sniffed and goes "That's how I like them". That's why they call him Animal. Mick told me. D'you think it's true?'

The little Makeup Girl looked up at Cass with serious eyes. For a moment Cass was shocked – thirties was *old?*

'Some men are like that, I guess.' Some men were worse. Some men chopped up your heart inside your body, dragged it out piece by piece and trampled on it, if you let them.

'Men!' the Makeup Girl shrugged. 'They're all a bunch of wankers.'

'Yeah,' Cass agreed. She could hear Mac's gravelly laugh behind her. Even Mac had been married once, a long time ago.

'Are you a natural redhead?' asked the Makeup Girl, casting a professional eye over Cass.

'More or less.' More less than more these days.

'Let me give you a make-over this afternoon? A good foundation can make you look five years younger.'

'Why would I want that?'

'Depends if you want to find yourself a new man after your break-up.'

'Not a break-up, a divorce. It's not just about splitting up your old DVDs and vinyl collection; it's about losing your home, your car, your dog.'

'I'm sorry about your dog. Didn't know.'

'Thanks,' said Cass. 'Actually, there wasn't a dog.'

'What the hell's that noise?' shrieked Jimbo, running up behind them.

'What?' Cass said.

'That rustling, crashing, *dangerous* sort of noise?'

'I can't hear anything?'

'Open your ears,' said Jimbo, flapping his arms toward the

undergrowth flanking the path. 'Something's over there. This *is* the Brecon Beacons, isn't it?'

'So what?' Cass was mystified.

'Didn't you see that thing about the Beast of Brecon? A great big black – thingy?'

'Don't be ridiculous –'

'I saw it on the News,' said Mac. 'And the Gaffer swore blind he'd seen something when they were up here on a recce.'

The little Makeup Girl turned pale beneath her freckles and pulled Cass's arm closer.

'Mind you,' said Mac, 'turns out it was a big hairy dog…' Mac's story died in her throat with a rasping wheeze as two dark shapes burst out of the bracken and ran straight across the path in front of them. A stag and a doe leapt into the sunlight, then veered off, vanishing into the nearest patch of undergrowth. The dangerous sort of noise faded into silence. Something wild and beautiful was gone in an instant.

'Not the Beast of Brecon, then,' said Cass.

'Jesus! If I ever get back to civilisation I'll never complain about muggers and murderers and terrorists,' said Jimbo. 'I never want to see the countryside again.'

'Me too,' Cass agreed, though she wasn't much looking forward to whatever was awaiting her back in Greenwich. She'd left her half-refurbished flat in the hands of builders and her car in the hands of her ex-husband. She knew she should have fought harder to hold onto the things that mattered. She was going to miss that Skoda.

'Come on, taxi's waiting – and the hotel, a hot bath and the *loo*…' Picking up speed, she slid the last few feet down to the car park on her backside. Somehow she managed to transfer even more mud onto her face as she struggled to her feet.

'You OK?' asked the Makeup Girl. 'Right then, we'll go for the full makeover this afternoon.' And Cass lacked the strength to argue with her.

Chapter 2

South East London

The view from the window over Stonely Hill was dull, grey and noisy. Declan hardly noticed the noise anymore but the fumes from rush hour traffic slipped in through cracks and gaps between the concrete and Crittal frames. It all went to make up part of the hospital smell that hit you on the way in and clung to your clothes for the rest of the day. Declan had stopped noticing that too, except on Monday mornings for a few seconds at the start of a working week.

Case studies: lycanthropy, schizophrenia… The phone rang, and he ignored it, continuing to work on the laptop, snatching a few moments before the usual round of patients began to trickle in.

'Dr O'Neil, it's Dr Frawley – he's had to cancel, can you take his 11 o'clock clinic?' said Marge, poking her head round the door.

'What?'

'Dr Frawley, he's had to cancel. Could you juggle your 10 o'clocks and fit in some of his 11 o'clocks – we can send half of them home? The others would have to wait another hour, but surely that's better –'

'Where's Frawley gone off to this time?'

'Of course, I could send them all home – several of them are here already. I can phone the rest.'

'No, show me his list.' Declan saved and closed the *Lycanthropy* files and pushed the laptop across the desk to Marge, who brought up Frawley's patients and Declan's side by side – with a bit of juggling he'd be able to see most of them. Marge swiftly deleted one of Declan's own patients from this morning's appointments.

'What happened to Joe?' Declan asked.

'Got himself arrested again; his probation officer phoned in. He was screaming outside Woolwich Police Station all night long that he was going to kill himself and wanted to be put under section, but no one took any notice, so he broke their windows. He'll be back next month. It's all just attention seeking.'

'Well, he's got my attention, if no one else's. Fit him in as soon as.'

Marge laughed and went back to reception.

Declan pulled the laptop back across the desk and opened his research files again. Fifteen minutes not to be wasted. He selected *Lycanthropy Presentation* slide show and began to run through the sequence – six patients who think they are wolves; four patients who think they are dogs; two who firmly believe they are cats; one tiger – now that was a really scary delusional schizophrenic, tattooed over most of his body; and one gerbil.

The door squeaked in that annoying way it always did

whenever it opened all by itself, or as if by some ghostly hand of ages past. Declan ignored it. But this apparition was solid flesh and blood.

'Good morning, sunshine!' said Ted Heany, walking into the office and, sitting down on the desk, glancing at the laptop. 'Would you look at that?' he snorted, 'I keep telling you there's no mileage in animalistic delusions – you need to come up with a serious research topic –'

'Thank you, Ted, nice to see a colleague taking an informed interest in my work. Is that coffee for me? Thanks.' Declan took the cup Ted offered.

'God, this stuff's awful.' He drank it anyway.

Ted scrolled though the presentation notes, with a grin on his face. 'Wasn't this going to make your name before you were thirty?'

'Forty, before I'm forty.'

'You better get a move on, Dec – if this presentation is going to be ready for the *Psychiatry Today* dinner you've got less than a month.'

'Will you stop reminding me of that? What are you doing here anyway?'

'It's the first week of the month – time to pay my dues to the dear old NHS.'

'Is it today already? I'd forgotten. Look, you couldn't help me out? I've had to take on Frawley's appointments, he's off sick again.'

'Old man Frawley? Probably on the golf course. Sorry no, I've a very tight schedule – back to Harley Street straight after lunch, appointments all afternoon. Dinner at the Carlton with Jonas Simmons from Blonde pharmaceuticals tomorrow. They're launching some new trials – this is big, it's going to be the new chlorpromazine – anyone who's in on it from the start could make a killing. Ditch the old lycanthropy study; get in on the drug trials. Better still put Wolfman and Co into the trials. Good God, man, you don't even need to write the paper yourself, they provide a ghost writer. All you need to do is verify the data.'

'Thanks, but –'

'Think about it Declan: Harley Street – or NHS; private practice – or Sunshine Day Centre. You still driving the old Fun Bus for the day patients? You're worth more than that.'

'Nice of you to say so. I'll think about it. Really, I will. Once I've finished the lycanthropy paper.'

'You do that. Right, I'm off.' Ted paused for a moment in the doorway. 'And how is Rabbit Boy? Still hopping about the wards winding you up?'

'Rabbit Boy has been excluded from the study.'

'Ciao!' said Ted shutting the door behind him with a bang. Some plaster flaked off the wall and fell onto the grey carpet as the intercom buzzed.

'Dr O'Neil, could you pick up Dr Frawley's patients' notes? I wouldn't ask, but I can't leave reception – I've got a queue forming,' came Marge's voice.

'No problem,' Declan replied. No chance to get any more writing done before the morning's clinics began anyway. He snapped the laptop shut.

Declan stepped out of the office. Ahead of him he could see Ted's Armani suited rear disappearing round a corner towards the office he used on his monthly visits. In the corridor were the usual rows of patients sitting waiting. The man in grey with dull eyes: a depressive, or just plain bored with waiting and nothing to read but old copies of *The Lady*? That thin middle-aged woman clutching a handbag tightly to her flat chest, the way she kept stretching her neck to peer round the corner to check the clock told you she was desperate to get out of this place. And who wouldn't be? This hospital was old, ugly and in need of more than a lick of fresh paint. Maybe Ted had been wise to set his sights on the Holy Grail of Harley Street right from the get-go.

A young black woman, smartly dressed, holding a big floppy hat on her lap, was chattering a non-stop stream of French into the air, oblivious to everyone around her. Declan smiled at the little girl by her side, holding tight to her mamma's hand. She stared shyly at him and giggled as if they were doing something naughty and shouldn't really be there at all. The child hadn't a clue what was going on, at her age this must have seemed like some strange new game. Declan wondered why social services hadn't been called to take her – perhaps they were on their way? Maybe it was best to leave her with her mother for now; though where her mother had gone to, she couldn't follow.

He could see it was going to be a long morning. *Lycanthropy and Schizophrenia – a new series of case studies for the 21st Century* would be on the back-burner a while longer. So what? After all, the *Psychiatry Today* presentation wasn't till the end of the month. He had more pressing work to do here today.

Chapter 3

The Tulpa

'You look great,' said Neil, the Director, speaking over a glass of red wine. 'What have you done to yourself?'

'When I'm not stuck halfway up a Welsh mountain freezing my socks off, I do sometimes risk wearing a frock.' Cass didn't mention the five-years-younger makeover that had taken up much of the afternoon.

'Well, sweetheart, you should do it more often. Now, about tomorrow morning –'

'Everything's sorted Neil: caterers, extras – same extras as yesterday, no nasty surprises for wardrobe, and transport assures us the new coach will be fine.'

'Wonderful, we're going to have to get you on the next job, Cass, you're too good to let go.'

'What next job would that be?' asked Cass warily. Not another low-to-no budget indie, please.

'We've landed the *DayDawn* account,' smirked Neil. 'Shampoo commercials – real money.' And he wandered off to refill his glass and throw his arms around someone else. All goodwill and charm tonight; tomorrow morning he'd be like a bear with a sore head.

Bloody stupid idea to go ahead with the wrap party tonight when they hadn't even wrapped, especially when they had to be out again at 4 a.m. to set up. Having spent a tedious good while re-organising the schedule, re-booking rooms, supporting artistes, transport, and caterers, Cass could have done with an early night. The afternoon make-over hadn't been too awful – though the eyebrow waxing was a bit eye-watering. It's ridiculous when you think of it, over a lifetime you must pluck, wax and depilate enough superfluous bodily hair to stuff a double duvet and still end up sleeping alone. Who was it who said that? Joan Rivers?

'What did Neil want?' asked Animal, appearing at her side.

'Wants me to work on *DayDawn* shampoo commercials.'

'No shit? You should bite his hand off! I would.'

They pushed their way through the crowd around the hotel swimming pool, heading for the barbeque provided by the hotel, and cheap plonk provided by the sparks. One glass of wine and some spare ribs was all she wanted, then bed. The noise of a rather crackly speaker system was rasping out some old Bonnie Tyler song about a total eclipse, and her head was beginning to ache.

Animal slipped an arm around her waist. 'This is our dance, Flash,' he said, dragging her towards the pool side. 'You look good enough to eat this evening.'

'Piss off, Animal,' said Cass, giving him a good shove with any luck should have sent him into the pool. He teetered on the edge and righted himself again.

'Don't be like that!'

'Fuck off, I'm going to bed,' said Cass and headed for her room.

'The party's only just beginning – you can't go now…'

But she could and she did, as Animal's voice faded into the background.

*

The ground floor hotel room was overheated and stuffy. Cass wanted to throw open the windows and let in some fresh air but there wasn't any out there, only the lingering miasma of charred meat and cigarette smoke, mixed with a whiff of cheap wine and beer. She went to the sink to take a couple of soluble aspirin in a glass of water. She splashed her face and wiped away a dark smudge of eye shadow on the hand towel and noticed that she still wore the faint ghost of a wedding ring, a white scar running around her finger. That too would vanish, given time. Better try to get some rest now.

The steady thump, thump, thump of music resonated through the floor. Every time she put her head to the pillow she could feel the bass rhythm scrambling her brain. Why did every unit party she'd ever endured have to end with Boney M and Donna Summer? Were they all stuck in a disco time-warp?

It was hopeless trying to sleep with all that going on, maybe reading would help. She picked up her script notes and browsed through them. Something about the whole improbable *tulpa* story intrigued her. The Tibetans had always believed in the power of a living thought form with an existence in the real world, independent of its creator. But there were Westerners, like Alexandra-David Neel, and others, who also claimed to have created them. There was even a photocopy here of a magazine article about some woman who claimed to have accidentally created a wolf *tulpa*.

A sudden sharp knock on her window made Cass jump. She turned around as Animal's face appeared, smiling, and waving a bottle of wine and two glasses. She went over and opened the casement enough to grab the wine bottle and pull it inside. She tried to close the window, but already Animal's shoulder was in the way.

'Aw,' he whined, 'can't I come in?'

'Go away. I've got to be up again in a couple of hours.'

'Hardly worth going to bed, is it? Get some of that down you, you'll soon feel better!' He straddled the windowsill, one leg in her bedroom, and handed her a wine glass. Then he tried to swing his other leg over the sill.

'What part of 'no' don't you understand?' she hissed, rapping him sharply on the knee.

'You are giving out very mixed signals, lady,' he complained, but swung his leg back over the sill and sloped off. Cass closed the window and pulled down the blind. One more glass of wine wasn't going to do her any harm…

*

Later, lying on top of her bed, after the one or two glasses that turned out to be one too many, Cass tried to ignore the throbbing in her head, and think instead of coolness: fresh, cool mountain streams, snowy white Arctic winters, faraway regions of glaciers and permafrost and brief, fast flowering summers. Surely global warming couldn't really melt all of that away, just as this hot, stuffy, annoying room was melting her away?

She began to feel like she had the flu, dozing in restless fever dreams. Her arm drooped down towards the floor. And in her weary brain a bubble of anger and frustration began to form an idea. What was it that woman in the magazine article said she had created by the power of thought alone? A werewolf? A great big timber wolf… a Beast of Brecon…

She began to flesh out a nightmarish shape of sinew and bone and blood. Something strong and supple, fierce and fearsome, that could run free in the cold moonlight of an Arctic night, feeling the call of the winds that sweep across the tundra. Whether she dreamt it, or it dreamt her, she was never quite sure, but as her hand fell over the side of the bed, she felt her fingertips graze the thick, harsh fur of something that growled softly at her touch. It seemed almost real.

Cass offered her hand to be nuzzled and the wolf licked her palm. Its tongue was warm and gentle. This was her dream-wolf, it would do whatever she wished. It was her creature, something wild and beautiful, waiting to be set free to make mischief.

'Good wolf, nice wolf – see 'em off!' she hissed, and the wolf leaped to its feet, gave itself a quick shake like a pet dog, then launched itself towards the closed window, sailing straight through the glass like a moon shadow.

*

The party outside was degenerating into various kinds of bad behaviour that Cass could only guess at, as she lay on the bed, eyes closed. But she was slightly surprised to hear the rowdiness turn to gasps and screams, and even a splash as something large and heavy fell into the pool. The loud cussing and swearing that followed seemed to be coming from Animal. And the music stopped.

Outside her window she thought she could hear Jimbo and Mac's voices, as they hurried by. Mac was muttering something about 'bloody great Alsatian dog like that, shouldn't be allowed in the hotel', whilst Jimbo was saying something like 'Help!'

Although red wine and exhaustion were finally working their sleepy magic, Cass pulled herself up to peer out of the window into the smoky darkness. And what she thought she saw across the patio, now deserted, was indeed 'a bloody great Alsatian dog' running towards the wall at the far end, where it leapt into the air and melted through the brickwork like a wraith. Then she slipped back down into a fitful, drunken sleep. But somewhere through her dreams she seemed to hear the faint pulse of a wolf heart beating slightly faster than her own close by. But by dawn's early light all would be forgotten in one hell of a hangover, and back to work.

Chapter 4

Desiderata

There must have been a day when *Desiderata* came down off the wall, along with a tattered poster of that show she'd once directed at university, to be replaced with the recipe for playdough and a weekly schedule of family activities; but for the life of her Alison couldn't remember when. She ticked off Monday and looked at the days to come – dental appointment for the twins after school, pick up Ted's suit from the dry-cleaners, make baked goods for school fete. Why had she said 'yes' to that?

It was 6 a.m. half an hour to herself before breakfast, time to get the first pile of washing into the machine. Alison loaded up the Bosch and set the wash programme to 'Acrylics'. No Acrylics were harmed in the washing of this laundry, she thought to herself.

'Allie! Where's my suit?' came a cry from above. She really didn't like the tone of that voice; already it implied fault finding rather than a genuine enquiry.

'Which one?' she called back.

'My blue, the one I'm wearing for the dinner with Simmons this evening?'

'That would be your blue suit that's at the dry-cleaners?'

'*What?*'

'It went to the cleaners after one of the twins was sick all over your trousers?'

Ted appeared in the doorway, in bathrobe and slippers, holding out two ties in one hand and two shirts in the other.

'So what am I going to wear?' he said. She still didn't like that tone.

'Wear your grey Paul Smith – and the Dior tie, with the pink stripe shirt.' Alison shrugged. If only everything in life were that easy.

'All right – but I must have the blue one back for tomorrow night.'

'What's tomorrow night?' Alison felt a slight panic rising, was there something that had been missed off the schedule? Should she be getting her hair done, arranging babysitters? Finding a semi-formal dress, or even a formal dress?

'Guildhall dinner – it's OK, you're not invited,' Ted said and disappeared.

Alison relaxed and scribbled *Ted's Guildhall dinner* on the schedule, then went upstairs to get the kids up.

Once Ted was out of the door with a quick kiss and a 'don't wait up', Alison made the twins' lunch boxes – only one savoury snack, one sweet snack, definitely no fizzy drinks, just water – and dressed Debbie in dungarees for Toddler Group. There might be sand and water play involved, even a walk if the weather stayed fine. She piled the three girls into the second-hand people carrier with the sticker that said *My Other Car's a Porsche*, which an old schoolfriend had sent her last Christmas. Actually their other car *was* a Porsche, but she didn't like to tell her friend, so she'd just laughed and stuck it in the back window and forgotten to remove it. This morning's school run meant only two neighbouring kids to pick up, because the Slater boy was down with something, and she hoped it wasn't catching, whatever it was.

*

Helping at Toddler Group took up the rest of the morning, then back home to make lunch for Debbie and putting her down for a nap, then a phone call to Ted's mum to make sure she knew what day of the week it was, which always took longer than anticipated. Then back to vacuuming the lounge, and putting on another lot of washing, before getting Debbie up again from her nap. The kitchen TV was pivoted towards her as she worked. Daytime TV and the nicotine patch on the inside of her elbow mostly kept her sane.

'Police are widening their investigation of the Deptford and Woolwich areas of docklands, after this third discovery of a young woman's body in the grounds of a disused factory. The body has not yet been identified but appears to have lain undiscovered for some weeks. As yet there is no confirmation of a link to the previous killings.'

She picked up the remote and hit the mute. She could watch the news headlines without hearing all the gory details. By now Debbie was absorbed with a colouring book at the kitchen table, as Alison stirred playdough mix in a saucepan on the ceramic hob. Five minute's peace. There would be time to nip into the dry-cleaners before the afternoon school run.

The doorbell chimed. She hated those fancy chimes, they always meant something bad waiting on the doorstep – must change them for a straightforward old fashioned ring tone that actually sounded like a doorbell.

'Don't touch anything, Debbie!' she called as she ran to open the front door. 'Cass! What are you doing here?'

Her sister was standing there with her old bike and a rucksack that must have first seen action back in her student days.

'Hello, Allie, nice to see you too,' said Cass.

'You're not bringing that bike in here – wheel it round to the garage.'

'It'll be OK out here for a minute, won't it? No one's going to steal bikes in this neighbourhood. They'll go straight for the BMWs, or nick the cat off granny's Honda.' Cass propped the bike up by the front porch and dumped her rucksack in the hall. 'Any coffee on the go?'

Alison put on the Nespresso, while Cass made a fuss of Debbie. Alison was a mite too slow to grab the bar of chocolate that Cass handed to the toddler, who began to stuff pieces into her mouth as fast as she could.

'Debbie! That's naughty – you know today isn't Sweetie Day. Say thank you to Aunty Cass and save the rest,' said Alison, removing the remains of the chocolate bar from Debbie's fist.

'Sweetie Day?' asked Cass.

'I'm trying to bring them up to have their own teeth. Anyway, what brings you here?'

'Well – oh, you're going to say: I told you so.'

'So, give me the pleasure?' said Alison, turning the ball of peppermint green gooey stuff out of the saucepan and onto a pastry board. She kneaded and stretched it as Debbie watched, carefully licking the last crumbs of chocolate from her fingers.

'It's that fuckin' useless plumber Barycz – sorry! My flat's a disaster area. The kitchen ceiling's come down. Muck and plaster everywhere. Could I stay here for a few nights? Won't take long; just till it's cleaned up?'

'Of course, you can,' said Alison, rolling out the dough, and cutting heart shapes with candy cutters. 'Can I say it now?'

Cass nodded glumly. Her fingers edged towards the pastry board.

'What do you expect when you get cowboy builders? I warned you – well, yes, I told you so.' Alison was certainly not feeling triumphant, merely justified.

Cass picked up one of the candy shapes and admired it.

'Don't!' said Alison.

'What? Do I have to wait for Sweetie Day too?' Cass popped it into her mouth.

'It's playdough – for Toddler Group.'

Cass spat out a gobbet of slimy green salty stuff into her hand. 'You might have told me. I thought it was a peppermint fondant.' She washed her mouth out with a swig of coffee and deposited the goo in the kitchen bin.

'*You* said you were going to phone me when you got home last night. I was worried about you,' said Alison.

'Why? We had an extra overnight, that's all.'

Alison picked up the local paper and pushed across the table. 'Deptford Wolf's Latest Victim' and 'Full Moon Killer Horror' ran the headlines.

'You must have seen it, even in Wales.'

'I live in Greenwich, not Deptford,' said Cass.

'I tried ringing you.'

'No signal up the mountain where we were filming.'

'You could have phoned from the hotel.'

'Sorry. Anyway, why are they calling him the Deptford Wolf?'

'God only knows. Full moon werewolf killer – how sick is that? I'd call him the Welling Weasel, or the Plumstead Plonker – they're always horrible, weaselly little characters when they get caught. Could be anyone's husband, brother, neighbour. All I'm saying is: be careful. When some bloke from the next flat comes round to borrow a jar of Gold Blend you want to slip the chain on the door.'

'Charming,' said Cass. 'Any more coffee? I've been up since 4 a.m. standing around on a Welsh hillside. Then I had to get a lift home with Animal.'

'Isn't that the creepy bloke you can't stand being around?'

'Yes, I *know*, but he has a van and he only lives down the road in Woolwich. I couldn't face taking the train back. I'd have my own car if my fuckin' useless – sorry – ex-husband didn't still owe me for the Skoda, and my flat's going to take weeks to get sorted.'

'Debbie, time to go and watch Paddington,' said Alison and took her off to watch TV in the lounge. When she came back her tone was quite sharp. 'You said it wouldn't take long to finish work at the flat?'

'Well, probably not *that* long,' Cass back-tracked quickly, 'Got anything to eat?'

Alison put away the playdough candies in a plastic box. She pulled out the little olive wood bread board and began to cut sandwiches.

'I don't know what you're complaining about,' she said, 'at least you've got your career. I've been at home for five years and it feels like my brain's beginning to turn to boiled cabbage.' She pushed the bread board towards Cass, mentally stopping herself from cutting the crusts off the sandwiches as she would for Debbie.

'It was your choice to have children,' Cass pointed out, munching her cheese and pickle on organic artisan rye bread.

'That's exactly what Ted says – as if he had nothing to do with it.'

'You always wanted three, didn't you?'

'Not all at once! First the twins then Debbie so soon after – that was my dentist's fault.'

'Really?' Cass's sandwich hovered some way from her mouth.

'Didn't I tell you? When I had that abscess on my wisdom tooth? He put me on antibiotics, and I asked if it was all right to take them because I was on the Pill, and he said it was.

And it *wasn't.*'

'I had no idea.'

'Neither had the dentist.' said Alison. She glanced at the clock. 'Is that the time? I have to pick up the twins from school, they've both got dental appointments – no, not him, we went private after that. Cass, do me a favour? Nip down Blackheath village and get me a couple of things? Oh, my God, I was supposed to pick up Ted's suit from the drycleaners. Can you carry it on your bike without damaging it?' She scribbled a list and found a crumpled dry-cleaners ticket in her purse.

'I'll do my very best not to,' said Cass. 'Give me the ticket.'

'Mummy!' called Debbie from the lounge, 'Want Peppa Pig! Can't get Peppa Pig! Don't want fuckin' useless Paddington Bear!'

'*What* did you say, Debbie Heaney?' said Alison, giving her sister a very hard stare.

'I'm on my way!' And Cass was out of the door, vowing to clean up her language around Alison and the kids.

Chapter 5

Psychic Self-Defense

Cycling across Blackheath on a sunny afternoon would be quite pleasant really, if the working day hadn't begun sometime in the wee small hours in rural Wales. She'd had to steel herself to accepting a lift from Animal in his filthy white van. But he'd not been too objectionable; too tired and hung-over to grunt more than a few monosyllables all the way home. There was a livid bruise on the side of his face – must have bumped into something last night, though he said he couldn't remember.

Alison could have been a bit more welcoming. All this stuff about the Deptford Wolf had really rattled her cage. As if her exquisite Smallbone-kitchen-electric-aga-Rotarian-coffee-morning world was coming under siege from the forces of darkness. Blackheath isn't Deptford, thought Cass, as she parked her bike outside the mini-market.

She walked along the fruit and veg aisle and glanced at the pyramid of round, green cabbage heads. Each pale green globe was about the size of the wretched cowboy plumber Barycz's head, with its balding dome and comb-over. For a moment Cass lingered and thought how nice it would be to take a kitchen cleaver to his head and shred it like a crisp cabbage salad. No more than he deserved for the mess he'd made of her flat. But Alison's list directed her towards organic courgettes and aubergines, away from cabbages and thoughts of justifiable homicide.

As she paid for the veg, Cass found a scrap of paper in her pocket with a book title scribbled on it: *Psychic Self-Defense*. Defense with an S. It was by that American woman who'd accidentally created a wolf *tulpa*: Dion Fortune. And Blackheath's oldest bookshop was only a little way up the hill from the mini-market.

The bookshop sat on the edge of the heath, big plate glass windows overlooking the little church on the green. The windows were full of old prints and charts, and a few rare books. This was always one of her favourite places. You could find all sorts of oddities on top of the stacks at the back. Cass parked her bike again and went inside.

'I wonder if you could help me?' she asked the elderly bookseller at the counter. 'I'm looking for this.' She showed him the title written on the note. 'Or anything else by Dion Fortune?'

He directed Cass to the rear of the store and wandered off into some back room where he might have something amongst the unsorted books. Cass squeezed down the narrow aisles, finding her way blocked by an anxious looking middle-aged woman and a young man. As she brushed past with a quick apology, she noticed that the man – barely more than a spotty teenager – was deftly sliding books under his leather jacket. She hesitated, then decided it probably wasn't any of her business, and hurried on down towards the *Paranormal*.

Cass took the ladder to the top shelf, her fingertips reaching out as far as she could – and there it was in her hands. *Psychic Self-Defense*. Original dust jacket. 1960s reprint. And only £9.99. Success! Pausing at the top of the ladder, she had the odd sensation that she was being watched. Glancing through the windows all she could see were empty pavements, a white van and a couple of cars slowly driving by and beyond that the open heath where children played. And in the distance, something like a big grey dog running towards the park gates. No one was watching her at all.

Cass climbed down and headed back to the counter. Now she found her way blocked by several browsers: a couple more middle-aged women, that spotty teenage boy, a large man in a checked shirt and a tall, rather good-looking man she hadn't noticed before, though she must have walked right past him on her way to the stacks. He held the spotty teenager by the arm and was gently extracting books from beneath the boy's leather jacket, where Cass had seen them disappearing earlier. Like a conjuring trick the books re-appeared one by one, were passed to the first woman, then on down the line to the large man in the checked shirt, who re-shelved them. No one seemed to notice Cass.

'How are you getting on?' the bookseller called from the next aisle. He must have crept silently out of the stockroom, passing unseen between the tall bookshelves.

'No problem, I've found what I was looking for,' said

Cass. She hurried down the aisle, as the book-conjurer turned and saw her. He had a kind, slightly rumpled sort of face. He smiled at her with the recognition that he'd been rumbled. He didn't appear as guilty as she might have expected. Cass couldn't help grinning back, she'd realised by now that the bunch of browsers – the middle-aged women, the sulky teenage boy, the big man with the institution haircut – were all with him. A carer, that's what he was, from one of those places for people with learning difficulties. He was probably Romanian or Lithuanian, that's what they usually were these days. Probably an engineer or a doctor with a family to support back in his home country and she didn't want to get him into any trouble.

She had to squeeze past him on her way to the counter, with a quick 'sorry' as she almost tripped over his toes. She dropped her book on the floor and the nice man retrieved it for her.

'Sorry, sorry,' said the man, 'here you are – oh, *Psychic Self-Defense*, an interesting choice of reading.' And the accent was an attractive Irish brogue. Those blue-grey eyes and strawberry blonde hair with the slightest fleck of grey should have given her a hint of Celtic blood. He handed Cass the book with a smile, then turned back to his group.

'Thank you,' she said, and went to pay at the counter. What a lovely man... For a moment she had a strange notion that she'd seen him somewhere before, but where? Or when? No idea.

She was halfway across the heath, when she remembered Ted's suit at the dry- cleaners and had to turn back for it. She collected his suit, nicely folded in its Gold Service bag, balanced it on her handlebars, and cycled slowly back up the hill.

As she passed Costa she noticed the Irishman and his little group sitting outside having coffee. And she smiled to herself, wondering if he realised what she had observed from the counter as she paid for her *Psychic Self-Defense*. After the last of the teenage boy's stolen books had been re-shelved, Cass saw one of the nervous, middle-aged women flick several picture postcards out of a display rack and slip them neatly into her open handbag. The woman had shot a look of defiance at the lad, as if to say: *that's how you do it!* Cass wondered if the nice-looking Irishman had any idea what really went on behind his back.

Now she was dying to get back to Alison's to put her feet up. She hadn't used this old bike for quite a while. Cycling up from her flat through Greenwich Park to Blackheath hadn't been too bad, except for the weirdest feeling that she was being followed by something or someone that she couldn't quite see in the leafy distance. That feeling you have when someone's staring at you, like that strange moment at the top of the ladder in the *Paranormal* section. As if there's something there you can't quite catch out of the corner of your eye. Just tiredness, that's all it was. It had been a very long day. No point getting spooked. The way Allie had let the Deptford Wolf business get to her was ridiculous. No kind of wolf would disturb her dreams tonight as she snuggled down in Alison's immaculate guest room. And there would be hot croissants and coffee in the morning…

Chapter 6

The Savant

'So how are things going with the kleptomaniacs and obsessive compulsive disorders?' Dr Weiss asked, leaning back in his chair. Declan always found these visits to his analyst and mentor relaxing. Dr Weiss was one of the old school, he took an eclectic approach to psychiatry; he'd been around in the days when the preferred therapy at one well known Humberside hospital was an outdoor hockey match come rain or come shine – and who's to say it didn't work, as he often reminded Declan.

'OK, I think I'm making progress,' he replied.

'And I hear you're very popular at the Sunshine Day Centre,' said Dr Weiss. He took a biscuit from the plate on his desk, dunked it in his tea and sucked on it. His wife always brought them tea and biscuits as part of the ritual.

'Someone has to do it, but I can't quite put my finger on whose idea it was that it should be me.' In fact, Declan had a damn good idea it was old Frawley, but what was the point of making a fuss?

'Do you often feel that you are being manoeuvred by forces outside your control?'

'You mean like the NHS... Inland Revenue... my mother?'

'You haven't added your rabbi, your priest or your analyst to that list.'

Declan laughed and took a biscuit that tasted sweet and buttery. 'You'll be telling me you *don't* believe there are forces out there beyond our control,' he countered.

'And how's your research project going?' asked Dr Weiss.

Declan sighed and stared into his teacup. This was always the tricky bit – if he admitted to no progress then Weiss would want to know why he was self-sabotaging his chances of publication, success, promotion; if he suggested that he was making real progress then Weiss would gently probe for details. Declan would then give an outline of the latest developments and watch his mentor's eyebrows slowly edge their way up his forehead and disappear into the general wrinkles. He wouldn't necessarily express scepticism or even amusement as such. He didn't need to.

'It's coming along.' Declan said. That didn't sound too negative or too overconfident. 'I'll be giving my presentation at the end of the month.'

'Good, good, I'm looking forward to it. We all are.'

Declan smiled and tried to appear relaxed, though the knots were already tightening in his stomach at the thought of it. He was no public speaker. He didn't own a dinner suit; Marge had booked him a fitting at some posh dress hire place. The appointment card was still in his pocket.

'So, I'll need to read up on lycanthropy – Freud, Adler, or Bram Stoker?' the old man chuckled at his own joke. Declan smiled again, he'd heard that one before, in fact he heard it several times over the past few years, whenever his famous research paper had threatened to be ready for publication and missed yet another deadline.

'No, that would be vampires, not werewolves,' he said, 'You'll agree that the wolf is one of our oldest and most powerful archetypes – look at the Norse legend of Fenris Wolf, monstrous offspring of a devil and a giantess, so dangerous that the gods were forced to bind it with an invisible cord made of the footfalls of cat, the beard of a woman, and the power of true love. But Fenris Wolf didn't trust them and demanded that one of them put his hand in his jaws while they placed the leash round his neck. Tyr, the god of battles drew the short straw – and placed his own hand in the beast's mouth as a sign of good faith'

(Later on when he checked in his old schoolboy copy of 'Myths of the Norsemen' Declan found that there were six impossible items crafted into the chain Gleipnir but none of those included the power of true love. What had he been thinking?)

'I know, I know,' sighed Dr Weiss, 'when the Wolf felt the magical noose tighten, it bit off the war god's right hand at the wrist. So much for good faith gestures.'

'Fenris Wolf is bedded deep in European culture,' Declan continued, 'always ready to escape given half a chance. And look at the case of the Beast of Gevaudan, in 1764 in France, near the town of Langogne –'

'Yes, yes, you've told me about that one too! And you, my

boy, could look up the Likkutei Amarim – the *Tanya*. See what Rabbi Schneu Zalman of Liadi has to say about the nature of the human soul: half animal, half divine, in constant tension. Surely your lycanthrope is just another metaphor for this struggle in the human psyche? The unconscious mind thinks in clichés. Man, or beast? Man-beast? Why do you never look to your own heritage and roots?'

'Which heritage would that be? My father's or my mother's? Remember what Philip Larkin said about your parents?'

'Do you want to talk about it?'

Declan laughed and shook his head. Enough ground had been covered over the years of analysis to make him comfortable in his own skin, as much as anyone can be.

'I have to be back at the hospital for a staff meeting at twelve, then down to the Day Centre for a small group session.'

'Good. Well, I'll be seeing you before the Big Night – so we'll have a little chat about how to 'calm the nerves'. I heard some very good tips on *Women's Hour* the other day – slow deep breaths before you commence speaking, all that sort of thing.' Dr Weiss brushed biscuit crumbs from his waistcoat and waved towards the door. Declan took his arm and helped him get out of the armchair. Sitting for any length of time always made the old fellow's joints stiffen up.

'Are you a regular listener to *Women's Hour*?' asked Declan.

'My wife has Radio 4 on all day. So, either I listen, or I take out my hearing aid. Secret of a happy marriage.'

They wished each other good bye, and Dr Weiss headed

down the corridor towards the kitchen. As Declan went out of the front door, he could still hear the friendly sound of Radio 4 in the background.

*

Things were not going well at the Sunshine Day Centre. Davy was late for Group – par for the course – Patsy and Angela weren't speaking to each other – this happened every other week – and Big Malcolm hadn't turned up at all. They sat in a circle, along with a new student nurse, waiting for Declan to take the lead. No one wanted to talk. Not about their problems anyway. They were more interested in the news – wasn't it terrible, another poor girl murdered by that 'Deptford Wolf' creature? Shocking isn't it? No wonder people don't want to go out of their own front doors anymore.

At least they were talking about their feelings, thought Declan, though they might not be tangential to kleptomania and compulsive disorders. Why not explore the general mood of paranoia in the hopes of dispelling a more personal sense of doom and gloom? That was certainly the way he was feeling after yet another a tedious staff meeting had overrun. Everything went round in circles and nothing ever seemed to go forwards.

The glass doors swung open and Davy appeared. He slumped down into one of the ancient armchairs that made a rude noise as it surrendered to his weight. He put his smartphone into his jacket pocket with a resentful glance at Declan. Rules of the group, no phones. Davy was barely sixteen, a school refuser with a penchant for stealing male grooming products from local chemists. He justified this by explaining that you got to look good – and smell good – to get yourself a girlfriend. So far the Lynx effect had not hooked him a girlfriend, but he had now been excluded from school, so that was some kind of a result for a boy who hated the classroom.

'I think them girls were all slags and were asking for it,' said Davy, coming into the Deptford Wolf conversation.

'How you can say that, Davy?' said Annie, a depressed young shopaholic who had recently joined the group. She was a quiet, gentle soul, currently on sick leave from the nursing staff in the main hospital. 'No one deserves to get killed.'

'One of them poor things was a pensioner in her own home,' said Patsy, pausing her knitting for a moment. Patsy had been coming to group therapy for a while now. Of Jamaican heritage, in her late fifties, she came up on the bus from Hither Green. She always had some knitting on the go, said it was better than therapy when you were in a stew. 'You want to get your facts right, young man,' she said.

'So, what do you think about the way this is being reported?' asked Declan, trying to steer the discussion away from personal comments. 'All this full moon werewolf nonsense?'

'It sells a lot of newspapers,' said Patsy.

'It does that,' agreed Declan,' but *four* attacks in two months, can't all be at full moon can they? It doesn't add up, does it?'

'Once in a blue moon it does,' said Angela, a kleptomaniac

who was responding well to therapy. She was a thin, middle-aged, middle-class woman from Blackheath, who had been referred by her GP as a 'heart-sink patient'. Meaning that his heart sank whenever he saw Angela walk through his surgery door clutching her oversized handbag in nervous fingers.

'What do you mean?' Declan asked her.

'A *blue moon* only happens when you have a full moon at the start and end of the month. That's what it means. Last month was a blue moon month.'

'That's when he started killing people,' said Annie with a shudder.

Declan was about to steer the session in a new direction when Big Malcolm appeared in the doorway, very late and very apologetic. Had a bit of trouble with the bus. By the time he was settled down in his usual place the session was nearly over.

'What d'you fink about it then, Malky?' asked Davy, 'This werewolf bloke thing?'

'I dunno,' said Malcolm, with a baffled expression on his broad face. Malcolm had been out of the army for a couple of years and was still struggling with civilian life. He did not talk about what had happened to him in the forces, apart from 'the sleeping trials'. He was never very clear about what 'the sleeping trials' entailed, but dated his current problems from them. He could be shy, even monosyllabic in public, but within the group he had begun to relax and join in discussions. Declan briefly recapped the 'blue moon' and the Deptford Werewolf story for Malcolm's benefit.

'Oh, yeah – but what's that go to do with werewolves? If you want to break into someone's house, or garden shed, you go round the back on a moonlit night, don't have to shine a torch, do you? Be in and out before anyone notices. My dad told me that.'

'Thank you, Malcolm, for that professional insight,' said Declan.

'I wanted to say something that happened to me,' said Annie softly.

'Yes?'

'My next door neighbour's dog died.'

'Ah that's sad,' said Patsy, pausing her knitting for a moment of sympathy.

'Yes. It was,' said Annie with downcast eyes that always looked close to tears.

Declan looked at her, hoping for something more.

'Yes, it was very sad,' Annie said, 'I took them to the vet to have it put down. She couldn't go on the bus because it was too old to go upstairs, and they won't let you have dogs downstairs.'

'That's not fair!' said Davy, an authority on what was and was not fair.

'So I drove them to the PDSA. They'll do it for free.'

'You did a good thing,' said Patsy, pausing her knitting again to stroke Annie's arm.

'Did I? It was only because the people on the other side complained to the Council about the barking she had to have it put down. I should have… I could have…' she shook her head and couldn't go on.

'That's – that's *so* not fair!' said Davy, words almost failing him too.

Malcolm had been listening in silence, his face growing darker and darker. He felt things deeply, empathy overwhelmed him, a kind of emotional synaesthesia where he became a channel for other people's unexpressed emotions. Before Annie could finish her story he jumped up and began punching the door with his fist.

'Malcolm!'

Malcom stopped at the sound of Declan's voice, looking in surprise at the hole he had punched in the door. The Day Centre doors were flimsy at best. 'Sorry…' he muttered, as Declan lead him back to his seat and asked the student nurse who had been sitting in on the group to go and fetch the First Aid Box and the Accident Book. The young chap had been looking pretty bored up to this point, now he got up and hurried off on his mission.

'Sorry,' said Malcolm. 'I got a bit upset. I hate cruelty to animals!'

'Yes, dear, we understand,' said Patsy.

'They wouldn't let me have a dog when I was kid. Because of my asthma. Or a cat – they're even worse. It's the fur.'

'What did you have?' asked Davy. 'A snake? A boy at school said he had a boa constrictor at home, and they fed it live mice.'

'Stick insects.'

'Stick insets? But they don't do nuffink!' said Davy scornfully.

Malcolm was becoming pink in the face as Patsy slipped a couple of stiches, then butted in: 'They do camouflage. Stick insects are the best in the world at camouflage – except for the Dead Leaf Butterfly. They're also very good at camouflage. If there was a stick insect and a Dead Leaf Butterfly on a twig you wouldn't see either of them – you would just see a twig.'

'You're making that up,' said Davy.

'No, I'm not. I watch a lot of CBeebies with my grandkids,' said Patsy, 'it's amazing what you can learn. You should try it, young man. You might learn something too.'

By now Declan had patched up Malcolm's fist and entered a report in the Accident Book, which was on its way back to the ward with the student nurse. 'Now, I think our time's just about up, unless anyone else has something they'd like to share? Yes, Davy? Did you want to say something else?'

'Yeah, next time we have an outing in the Sunshine Bus can we go to Brighton? I like the seaside. You can get a good suntan at the seaside. Girls like that, don't they?'

'If we've finished, shall we go down to the little café for a cup of tea?' said Patsy, stuffing her knitting back into the bag, 'Will you come with us, Doctor? You look like you could do with a cuppa.'

Declan had to agree, he could do with a cup of tea – or something stronger – at the end of the working day. And who's to deny the therapeutic benefit of tea and biscuits and a chat?

Chapter 7

Storm Warning

Abreakfast with Alison's family was an organised breakfast. The twins, neatly turned out in bottle green prep school uniforms, ate spoon sized Shreddies while Debbie messed around with own brand Rice Pops, and Alison nibbled a reduced fat croissant with decaff coffee. Most mornings Ted was already gone by the time Cass got downstairs. This early in the morning she could face nothing stronger than half a pink grapefruit and a coffee, fully caffeinated.

'Come on girls, we're going to be late again,' said Alison, trying to get the twins to speed up. 'Cass, could you keep an eye on Debbie while I do the school run?'

'No problem.' It gave Cass time to wake up properly, check her emails, and have another coffee. When Cass switched TV channels to pick up the breakfast time news and the image of the latest Deptford Wolf victim filled the screen, she quickly switched back to CBeebies for Debbie.

Once Alison had returned from the school run and whizzed Debbie off to Toddler Group, Cass plucked up courage to cycle down to her flat to see how things were going. It wasn't the thought of the journey through Greenwich Park, where the Deptford Wolf might lurk behind every bush (pretty unlikely) nor yet the something else that seemed to shadow her every move (pure imagination). It was the thought of what might be waiting for her behind her own front door. Builders.

*

It was quiet – too quiet; where was everyone? They should be working. She strode into the kitchen, prepared for the worst and stopped. Not so bad. The old ceiling had already been replaced with new plasterboard to be papered and painted, the floor had been cleared up – the flooring would have to be replaced, Barycz was paying for that, too right he was!

She went across to the bedroom to collect a change of clothes – and screamed. The ceiling here was leaking in the corner of the room directly over her bed. Dirty brown water was still dripping steadily onto the bedframe. Her beautiful, soft, dreamy, fluffy, silk-stuffed, two hundred tog, king-size duvet (a wedding present from Ted and Allie) had turned it into a soggy giant teabag. It had been dumped against the wall, along with the mattress turned on its side. She might as well have let her ex take that along with all the other stuff she'd given up fighting over.

'Ah, I've been trying to get hold of you, Mrs Green!' There he stood in his coat and overalls with his plumber's bag, cheerful as ever. Mr Barycz, the evil little man. 'Didn't mean to startle you, just let myself in. We come up against a bit of a problem with the new heating system. Still leaking a bit, but we'll fix that. I moved your bedding out of the way soon as –'

'Look at it! It's ruined everything!'

'It's not as bad as it looks, just one of the old pipes up above give way. Couldn't take the extra strain. I hadn't got around to draining down the whole system before it went. One of the problems with these older conversions.'

'How long this is going to take to fix?'

'Oh, not more than a couple of days. Once we get the parts.'

'How long's that going to take?'

'Oh, not more than a week, once I get the order in.'

Cass could not trust herself to stay any longer. Rolling up the duvet and securing it with a couple of pairs of old tights, she told Barycz to go ahead and order the parts, and swept out cradling the duvet in her arms.

Balancing a waterlogged duvet over the handlebars was not easy. She cycled slowly along the streets to the main road, weaving in and out of traffic. A few large drops of rain fell on her face. Wonderful! By the time she reached the last run down laundrette in the neighbourhood she was soaked and thoroughly miserable.

Washerama was well past its heyday, shabby and little used. (These days you're lucky to find one at all.) The only other customer was a large man with a bad haircut sitting quietly on the bench, eyes half closed as he watched his smalls going round and round in the suds.

Cass's duvet plopped out of its bindings with a sigh, sagging over the wooden bench. She found a machine big enough to take it and began to stuff the duvet through the porthole door. It wasn't easy. King-size duvets are a two-man job at the best of times. In her hurry to get out of the flat before braining Mr Barycz, she had forgotten to bring any detergent, and now discovered she had hardly any coins in her purse. Who carries cash?

The big man had opened his eyes and was watching her. 'You can get some change from that machine on the wall,' he announced. 'It takes five pound notes.'

She thanked him and put in a fiver to collect a handful of pound coins. She bought herself a packet of detergent from the vending machine, then realised she still did not have the right combination of coins for the wash programme. The big man, who had been watching, summed up the situation for her. 'You'll need more change now!'

'Right,' said Cass, trying to smile, and searching her purse again found a solitary ten pound note. 'You couldn't change a tenner for two fives could you?'

It seemed to worry him, as if he was not totally sure that she could be trusted. Carefully and deliberately the big man checked his wallet, pulled out a couple of fivers and held them out to her. Cass handed him the ten-pound note. He looked relieved.

Cass got her coins, fed the washing machine and set the programme running. She sat on the bench at the far corner of the laundrette. She glanced across at the big man. There was something both oddly familiar and definitely odd about him, but you shouldn't be judgemental, should you? She lost herself in the pages of last December's *Cosmopolitan*.

*

Somewhere in the distance there was a rumble of thunder.

'I think we're going to get a storm,' said the big man. 'I said: I think it's going to storm,' he repeated. 'I don't like thunder and lightning.'

Cass looked up from her magazine. 'Oh, yes, it's gone really dark out there.'

By now her machine had spun to a final juddering halt, so Cass grabbed a plastic laundry basket and started to pull out the soggy duvet. It stuck fast in the porthole.

'Here, let me do it,' said the big man, shambling over. He wrenched the duvet out of the machine and into the basket with one hefty tug.

'Thanks,' said Cass, finding him rather too close for comfort. His clothes carried a faint whiff of mildew as if he'd been living down in a damp basement for some time. He was probably all right, but you never know? God, she was beginning to think like Alison! All that paranoia about the Deptford Wolf must be rubbing off. The man lifted her laundry basket and carried it over to the ancient spin dryer. With a powerful thrust he rammed the duvet inside and slammed the lid down on it with his fat fist. The lid clanged loudly with the force of the blow, and he grunted with satisfaction. 'You got fifty pence?' he said.

Luckily, she did. She put the coin in the slot and pushed the button. But nothing happened until he gave the machine a hefty kick with his boot, then it purred into action.

He beamed at her. 'Good job I was here!'

'Thanks,' said Cass.

'I come here regular. It used to be a nice place to meet people for a chat. There was Maggie, the lady who'd do a service wash for you. She was nice, she had a blue uniform, she was a *professional* – don't mix your whites with your coloureds, always give your duvet an extra spin – that was our Maggie. Now she's gone and they put a time lock on the door.' He sighed and lumbered back towards his own washing. The replacement of our Maggie with a time lock had clearly upset him.

A flash of lightening lit up the laundrette turning everything a sharper, colder shade of white, followed by a crack of thunder overhead. Then the lights went out – all the lights inside the laundrette, and all the shop lights along the street outside as far as the eye could see. Cass's spin dryer chugged to an unscheduled halt. The big man made a sort of whimpering noise. And the automatic time lock on the door tripped in.

*

Outside people were hurrying by, splashing through the pouring rain. No one was stopping to look at two people hammering on the windows of the laundrette.

'It's no use,' said Cass. 'We're going to be stuck in here for a while.' She looked around and spotted a contact number on the wall behind the tumble driers. 'We can phone for the owner to come down and open the bloody door.' She flipped open her phone case and started to dial. It was at this point she realised that she'd forgotten to put it on charge last night.

Emergency call only.

'Oh, you'll have to ring them. Have you got a phone?' she asked.

The big man shook his head. He hadn't got a phone. Some bad boys had nicked it off him. His breathing was coming slow and heavy now.

'The cleaning lady comes in the morning,' he said, 'she'll let us out, won't she?'

'We are not going to be here *all night*,' said Cass. 'I'll ring the Fire Brigade on Emergency call – don't worry, they'll get us out.' On the phone she tried to sound as genuine as possible, not like some idiot calling them out for the fun of it.

'When will they come?' asked the big man, pacing up and down.

'Well, being stuck in a laundrette isn't like a house fire, is it? We'll have to wait our turn.'

The big man was lumbering towards the door. 'Got to get some air!' he gasped, breathing heavily. He turned back and looked at her, red faced. 'You shouldn't bring dogs in here. No dogs allowed. I'm allergic to dogs. And cats. I got asthma.'

'What dog?' Cass looked at him stupidly. What on earth was he on about? What had dogs and cats and asthma to do with anything?

'It followed you in,' he said, pointing to the far corner of the laundrette.

She really didn't want to look in the direction his finger was pointing; she really didn't want to turn her head and see what was there. But she did look.

The wolf was lying on the floor amongst the plastic laundry baskets and the big man's abandoned washing. It was casually chewing up a sock. Even dream-wolves have a weakness for smelly socks, it seems. It had been there all the time, of course, glimpsed out of the corner of an eye, following her every step of the way from the Brecon Beacons, curling up in the corner of a bedroom, or in the back of Animal's dirty white van, running beside her through the park. Always a half step behind, a heartbeat away. The feral smell should have given it away; wet fur and something else.

It lifted its head and looked at her with sly, intelligent eyes and growled softly. It dropped the sock, lifting itself up onto its front paws, took one shake of the shoulders and launched itself into the space between the tumble driers and the door, heading straight for the big man.

'No!' Cass's scream was louder and longer than she imagined it could ever be, echoing around the metal appliances and the tiled walls. The wolf barely swerved but leapt right *through* the big man and sailed on through the plate glass window without breaking the surface. It twisted in the air, landed upon its paws in the rainy street, and ran off, fading into the distance. She saw it vanish, then turned back.

The big man was lying on the floor, gasping for breath. Cass tried to remember whatever she might have learned at that St John's Ambulance first aid course she'd attended. Where was the nearest defibrillator? Was there even a nearest defibrillator?

'Oh, God, please don't die, please don't die – I don't do

artificial ventilation, I can't even do triangular bandages properly... If you're asthmatic where's your inhaler? Why haven't you got an inhaler!'

'Forgot it...' He shook his head apologetically and looked as if he was about to burst into tears when she shouted at him.

'Now, come on, talk to me, talk to me – what's your name?'

'Malcolm, my name's Malcolm...'

'All right Malcolm, I'm going to ring for an ambulance, and they'll come really quickly – and the fire brigade. Yes, they'll be here too. Now I want you to breathe… slowly... in... out...' She tried breathing slowly with him, but found herself hyperventilating, so stopped that. She rolled him over on one side in the recovery position – not easy but achieved by using a towel from his washing basket. His face was puce and his breathing laboured, but at least he was still breathing. She must have got something out of that St John's course.

All the rest followed in a hideous blur: the fire brigade, ambulance, paramedics, embarrassing explanations, and slinking off back to Alison's with her duvet sagging across her handlebars. Good old Allie would know how to make things right again, anything from a damp duvet to a wolf *tulpa*; Alison would know how to fix it. She hoped.

Chapter 8

Come on Eileen

'It was all a hideous blur?' Alison regarded Cass with scepticism. They were sitting on the bed in the spare room – Cass's temporary bedroom– after supper. The kids were in bed, Ted was out at his Guildhall function, and they had the house to themselves. Alison had brought a couple of glasses and a bottle up to Cass's room, where they could drink in peace. She curled up on the bed, took a large sip of Prosecco and sighed with pleasure.

It had been a long day that had started badly. That morning Debbie had got into the bathroom before Alison had woken up and made 'potions': random mixtures of all the bottles she could reach down from shelves, or find in cupboards, swirled into a wonderful multi-coloured gloop in the bottom of the bath. Ted's expensive new aftershave was one of the casualties of Debbie's alchemical experimentation.

Ted was not best pleased when he went into the bathroom. He had shouted, and Debbie had sulked, and 'potions' were now on the banned list. Alison had to make peace and clean up the gloop, so that Ted could take a shower while she went downstairs to make breakfast. By the end of the day all Alison wanted to do was chillax, drink a cold glass or two, and watch something mindless on TV, rather than dealing with Cass's problems. She wanted to sympathise, but it wasn't always that easy. Her sister's problems tended to be a bit strange at the best of times, but not usually this weird.

'Now start again from the beginning,' said Alison.

Cass's story took a lot of swallowing, even in the retelling. The incident of the wolf in the laundrette and the big man with asthma still wasn't making much sense. Alison couldn't get a grip on it: obviously *something* had happened, but what exactly?

'Now each time my wolf appears it's bigger, stronger, more real,' said Cass melodramatically, 'I could have killed that man.'

'But he told you he had asthma, and the storm brought on an attack. You said he was scared of the lightening, so that was nothing at all to do with you.'

'So what about my wolf?'

'You said it was an *imaginary* wolf.'

'I said it was a creature born of my imagination – a *tulpa*. But *he* saw it too. And he had an allergic reaction to it.'

'That poor man was confused; you don't know what he saw – or thought he saw. Didn't you say you thought he was a bit odd? He could have been schizophrenic, or delusional? He could have been seeing pink elephants on parade for all you know! He might even have been dangerous,' said Alison. 'Anyway, you can't take responsibility for everything that happens around you.'

'Really? So what's that then?' demanded Cass, pulling the curtain aside. Alison followed her gaze and looked down into the moonlit garden below. There in the shade of the apple trees was that bloody great Belgian Shepherd dog from next door crapping on the grass.

'Oh for heaven's sake, Cass, that's next door's dog. I'll have to go and chase her out. She comes in through the fence and digs up my flowerbeds.'

'Are you sure?' Cass leaned out of the window and took another look.

'Yes. It's Mitzi – she's a Teveuren, a Belgian Shepherd.' Alison rapped on the window to frighten it away.

'Oh, well, from up here, in the dark you could easily take it for a wolf.'

Down below Mitzi howled in a passably wolf-like way, before running off to chase a neighbourhood cat. She scrambled through a narrow gap in the fence with no trouble, leaving behind a small memento on the lawn.

'I must get that fence fixed,' said Alison.

'You don't believe me, do you?' said Cass glumly.

'I believe that *you* believe it. And if you're convinced that you've created this wolf-*tulpa* thing and that it's haunting you, then so far as you're concerned it *does* exist. So you need to get it exorcised.'

'Exorcised? Oh, now you're having a laugh.'

'No, I mean you need some way to banish it from your mind.'

'Allie, am I going crazy? I don't want to end up off my

rocker in some pricy Swiss clinic like Zelda Fitzgerald.'

'Don't be so daft – have you got BUPA? No? I thought not. No one is going to fork out to send you to Swiss Cottage let alone a Swiss clinic. You'll go NHS and that could take months and months on a waiting list. You and your pet wolf could find yourselves banged up in London Zoo before then.'

'Allie, that is not funny!'

'No, it isn't; but I know someone who might be able to help you.'

'An exorcist?'

'A psychiatrist, you idiot. One of Ted's colleagues. He does some cash in hand work on the side.'

'One of Ted's friends strapped for cash? That's hard to believe of the Harley Street mob.'

'Ted's *only* friend. NHS, not remotely Harley Street. We were all at Uni together back in the day. He might be able to fit you in at short notice.'

'What do I need to do?'

'Ring this number,' Alison wrote a name and number on a yellow Post-it note from Cass's bedside table, 'it's his home number. Just say someone recommended him to you, but don't go into details.'

'OK. You're being a bit mysterious, but I'll give him a ring.'

'I think you'll like him; he's a really good bloke. And he's your only chance of seeing someone quickly. Don't lose that number.' Alison took another sip of wine and thought for a moment about her sister's mental state. She wondered what was really going on in Cass's mind; Ted would probably say it was all some kind of projection, whatever that meant. Then an idea struck her: 'Perhaps it's a poltergeist you know? That kind of energy thingy that attaches itself to teenage girls when all the hormones are running riot? Maybe with the divorce and everything you're having some kind of late onset oestrogen storm?'

'*What*? A poltergeist? I'd rather be plain nuts, thanks!' said Cass.

'Anyway, promise me you'll make an appointment?' Alison said. 'There's probably some perfectly rational explanation. If not, you'll get some pink pills to make it all go away! And *please* don't mention anything about this wolf business to Ted.'

'As if! The last thing I want is your husband's professional opinion.'

'You don't have to make it so obvious that you don't like him.'

'Sorry, Alison. But he'd only make me feel utterly stupid.'

'Yes, Ted can have that effect on people,' Alison had to admit. One day she might even tell him so to his face.

'OK, I'll give your bloke a ring tomorrow,' said Cass, sticking the yellow Post-it note onto the diary on her bedside table.

'Don't just say it – do it!' said Alison and went downstairs to check on Cass's duvet that was spread over four chairs in the utility room to finish drying out properly. Not for the first time she wished that everything in life was that easy to fix. The name she'd scribbled on the yellow Post-it note was 'Declan O'Neil.' Back in the day known to his old friends as

Dexy. She smiled and started to load the dishwasher, humming under her breath something that sounded like 'Come on Eileen'. A sweet memory of something that might have been, and a road not taken.

Chapter 9

An Invitation

Declan took another quick bite of the cold Cornish pasty that stood in for brunch this morning and scattered flaky crumbs over his desk. Very unprofessional, but he was starving. He scribbled a few notes on a small pad as he chatted with his new patient.

'I didn't mean to interrupt your lunch hour,' said the redheaded young woman, with the glow of sunlight from the dusty windows creating a kind of a halo effect around her hair. 'But I'm really grateful you could see me.'

'No, I'm only sorry I can't offer you a proper session till later in the week – but it's good to put a face to a name, Mrs Green.' She didn't appear to be in any great distress, he thought, and she had been vague about what was troubling her when she phoned him at 6 a.m. this morning. It was supposed to be some kind of emergency, but for the life of him he couldn't see why he was giving up his lunch break and a hot meal in the canteen for this brief meeting. However, he knew that people took time to open up and share their feelings, and it took time to build trust, so for now it was a dodgy pasty and cup of vending machine coffee at the desk for him. Not that he should be seeing her here at all, as Marge would no doubt remind him later. This was not an appropriate place for receiving private patients.

'Cassandra – Cass, please. And what do I call you? Doctor or Mister?'

'Declan will do fine. And what exactly brings you here?'

'The number 89 – as my ex got custody of the Skoda, and my bike has a flat tyre since I rode over some nails left outside my flat by the wretched builders, who've been in and out for two months now and still haven't finished the job. In fact, they've made things a whole lot worse.'

'And?' He prompted, cutting into her flow of annoyances. There must be more than unsatisfactory workmanship at the root of her problems otherwise she'd come to the wrong place for help. Checkatrade.com might be more appropriate.

'And my sister suggested you might be able to help me with…anger management issues.'

'Ok. Are you currently on any medication?'

'Apart from Rescue Remedy, Echinacea drops, Evening Primrose – oh, and St John's Wort? No, I'm not on anything. Oh, and Beconase spray for my hay fever.'

'I take it you prefer to work with alternative therapies?'

'Anything wrong with that?'

'Not at all. Though some people can have a reaction to some herbal remedies.' *Anger management* Declan noted on his scribble pad. His new patient did seem a bit irritable, though if what she told him about the situation with the cowboy builders was true, it might go part way to explaining her current mood. At that point the intercom buzzed through Marge's voice telling him that he had a call waiting from Dr Frawley.

'Put him on hold for a moment, Marge, we're almost done here,' said Declan, checking his desk diary. 'I have a free hour this Wednesday lunch time? I could come over to your flat?" He smiled at Cass and hoped she understood that he did not do consultations with private patients at the hospital.

She said Wednesday was fine, but *not* at her flat because that was a total disaster area, and she'd sort out a suitable place where they could meet for an hour. He gave her the little card with his mobile number for private patients. As she leaned forward to take it from his hand, her auburn hair fell across her face, and Declan had the odd feeling he'd met her before. It would come to him eventually. But for now, he had kept Frawley on hold long enough.

*

Another afternoon at the Sunshine Day Centre. Declan had come away from a long phone conversation with Dr Frawley about funding cuts that had left him feeling dispirited and hoping for something more positive to come out of this group therapy session. He sunk into the armchair that made rude noises, daring anyone to smile.

After a few odd tears and silences, and a baffling outburst about nothing in particular, the usual group settled down comfortably with Patsy doing her knitting (good sign or bad sign? Declan was never sure) and he even managed to encourage Annie to talk about herself and her work.

'I was on the geriatric wards – mostly old women,' she began quietly 'I remember one of them was so old she was curled up like a foetus in her bed, with a pink ribbon tying up her wispy hair. I was feeding her baby food from a jar, gooseberry fool, and she swallowed each mouthful carefully. Her arms and legs were drawn up into her body, bones as fragile as a baby bird that's fallen out of its nest. She was so old, so frail, but she wouldn't die; she just held on, tasting each tiny mouthful of gooseberry fool.

'Then there was another little old white lady who came in with a strange Afro hair do, but when we came to wash her hair we found that she'd pulled on one hairnet after another as her hair grew through it, making a kind of helmet, you know? We had to cut it all away until she looked like a shorn lamb. Then we washed her and bathed her until she came up all nice and pink and clean.'

'That's disgusting!' said Davy. 'Old people are smelly; they should bath themselves.'

'Oh Davy,' said Annie with a flicker of a smile, 'they can't help it. We have to try to give them back their dignity, though it's hard when there are never enough hours in the day,' she sighed.

'If it's such a rotten job I don't see why you want to do it,' said Davy.

'It's all I ever wanted to do, to be a good nurse. Now I can't even do that.'

'It's a poor mouse that only had one hole,' said Angela with a sniff. And Annie looked as if someone had slapped her round the face.

'Angela, that's not very helpful,' said Declan.

'Sorry, Annie, but it's true. You have a degree, you'll always be able to find your way in the future. Not the same for the likes of me. University was for my brothers – it would be wasted on me. I went to night school. And paid my own way.' Angela was certainly letting out a few of her feelings today.

'That's not fair,' said Davy. The sheer unfairness of the adult world he was entering always seem to shock him.

'No it wasn't fair, but that's the way it was,' said Angela.

'Everyone deserves an education, don't they Davy? They just have to seize the opportunity,' said Declan. Davy blushed and looked down at the ground and mumbled something that might have been a *yes*. Well, that was some kind of progress thought Declan.

He was about to wrap up the session when Big Malcolm finally appeared. Malcolm edged his bulk into the circle and looked round for somewhere to perch. For some obscure reason he was carrying a large plastic laundry bag in his arms.

'Take a seat, Malcolm,' said Declan, resigning himself to overrunning again.

'What's up, Malky?' asked Davy.

'Sorry I'm late, Doctor, I been down the Police station, 'cos I was at the laundrette the other day –'

'Here, did you rob a laundrette or somefink?' asked Davy looking impressed.

Declan made a gesture silencing Davy and encouraging Big Malcolm to go on, whilst the rest of the group began to sit up and take interest.

'I was at the laundrette the other day,' Malcolm repeated, 'when we had that really bad thunderstorm, and I got myself locked inside with a woman and a dog.'

'What's a dog doing in a laundrette?' asked Patsy.

'Perhaps it was a Guide Dog?' suggested Annie, still sniffing back a few tears.

'No, it wasn't a Guide Dog, it was an Alsatian, I think,' said Big Malcolm. 'But I had one of my asthma attacks and had to go into hospital in an ambulance.' Patsy, Angela, Annie and the other ladies of the group all reacted with sympathy and concern. Malcolm was a bit of a pet with them.

'Did you forget your inhaler again, Malcolm?' asked Declan, and was not surprised to see the big man look embarrassed and shake his head. The ladies of the group tut-tutted and looked at Malcolm as if he were a very large naughty schoolboy.

'And then somebody stole my washing from the laundrette,' said Malcolm. 'And I had to go to the police station to get it, 'cos someone had thrown it into one of the front gardens in Carnival Street. And the Police got it back, 'cos someone handed it in.'

'Who'd want your manky old washing? No wonder they chucked it away!' laughed Davy and was silenced with a look from Patsy.

'Funny thing was, the police give me the wrong bag at first, because it had a pair of trainers and a T-shirt in it and it said EVIDENCE on it. I said I didn't think it was mine, and the policeman laughed and said it was from a crime scene.'

'He's just winding us up!' said Davy. 'I don't believe it.'

'Be quiet, Davy,' said Patsy. 'You go on and tell us what happened, Malcolm.'

'I think it was from a murder,' said Malcom. 'There was blood all over the trainers, and the T-shirt was wrapped up round something that looked like a knife.' There was a reaction from all round as Malcolm paused for effect. 'Then the policeman took it away and gave me my bag of washing – *and it's all still here!*' He beamed at them over his salvaged laundry bag.

'Well,' said Patsy, taking a brief pause from her knitting, 'It don't give you much confidence when the police can't tell the difference between a bag of forensic evidence and Malcolm's smalls. I don't imagine they'll be catching this Deptford Wolf character anytime soon, do you?' And at that point it was time to call it a day.

*

Declan made a quick dash over to the office to pick up some notes and his laptop. He'd noted a couple of dates in his diary, picked up his gear, and was almost on his way home, when Ted popped his head around the office door.

'You still here?' Ted said. 'I'm off, till next month.'

'Nice work if you can get it! Ted, I've been meaning to ask you…'

'You've had second thoughts about the drug trials? Good man!'

'No, not yet. I'm still thinking about it,' said Declan as

they walked down the corridor towards the lifts.

'Aha, you want to discuss your miserable love life?' You want to screw one of your patients and want to know if its ethical?' Ted slapped him on the back.

'You really have this analysis thing down to a fine art, don't you?' said Declan.

'If you want my advice: it's unethical, unprofessional, out of the question. However, I could lend you the keys to my little cottage in the Dales, if you promised to be very discreet.' They stepped into the lift together and headed for the ground floor. The lift smelt of disinfectant and sour milk.

'Ted! Be serious for once. No, I want you to help me with the *Psychiatry Today* dinner – you know what I'm like with technology – if you help me set up, I'll feel a lot better. I bloody hate giving presentations. Death by PowerPoint holds a very personal meaning for me.'

'No problem. I'll hold your hand if you want me to – though there's no need to get agitated, it's not like it's your annual review. It's just another jolly for the publishers – they want their magazine to look good, they throw one of these bashes – pretty waitresses, good food and wine, and you provide a bit of a floor show. So long as you keep them entertained you'll be fine. Who's the other speaker?'

'That woman from the TV – the sexual problems programme – the one with the big earrings? She's giving a paper on Gaming Addiction.'

'If you really want to make a name for yourself invent a new addiction, that's what I always say! You should do something on *TikTok Rage* or – or *Instagram Envy*, though by the time you finish writing your paper, TikTok and Instagram will be as obsolete as Blackberries and Friends Reunited.' he laughed. 'Maybe you are safer sticking to your werewolves and zombies and vampires – they never go out of fashion. They just reinvent themselves for every new generation. Now, how about coming over to mine for dinner this Friday night, and we can talk through your presentation afterwards?'

Declan hesitated for a moment. 'Friday is your family night; I don't want to impose.'

'Friday night is *pie night*: steak and kidney, chicken and leek, shepherd's pie – lots of mashed potatoes, rich, thick onion gravy? Eat your heart out Nigella Lawson when my little Alison's cooking.'

'She was always a good cook,' Declan admitted, weakening at the thought of real food. 'OK. This Friday? You're on! Thanks.' And they stepped out of the lift and walked into the late afternoon sunlight of South East London as the traffic began ramping up for the journey home.

Chapter 10

Petrichor

Cass arrived at Alison's as the ladies of the Neighbourhood Watch were leaving. There were three or four 'yummy mummies', a grandma or two, and one skinny au pair in clogs.

'Hi Cass,' said Alison, 'you're back early. We've only just finished having our meeting. 'Bye, girls!'

'This is your sister, isn't it?' said Mrs O'Hanlon, 'Nice bit of company for you. Poor Marie-Claire is scared to stay in the house alone. I have to keep her company while my daughter's out at work and the children at school.'

'Everyone's at risk while that Deptford Wolf character is on the loose,' said Mrs McBride, the Belgian Shepherd owner from next door.

'I thought the papers said he only goes for prostitutes?' said Mrs O'Hanlon, hurrying the skinny au pair down the front path in front of her.

'High risk profession,' said Cass, casting a sardonic look at Alison.

'No, he's not fussy whoever he kills so long as it's a woman,' said Mrs McBride, shaking her head, and there was little more to be said. Alison waved goodbye and closed the door.

Cass wheeled her bike in through the side gate and left it propped up against the wall. She came into the kitchen through the garden door and was about to go upstairs when Alison barred her way.

'I heard that little crack you made about "high risk profession",' Alison said.

'What? Where's your sense of humour? Left behind when you moved to Blackheath and joined the Rotarians?' Cass couldn't see why Alison should be annoyed.

'They were one short of twenty – what could I say?'

'What happened to you, Allie? You were a rebel. You used to be in the Lewisham Anarchists when we were still at school?'

'That was only because they had access to a photocopier and I needed it to get my underground student newspaper started. And what about you? I can remember when you were plain old Carol Pratt before you went off to Uni, turned into *Cassandra*, and shaved off all your hair.'

'That was only for one term! I let it grow back when I realised it wasn't a such good look on me.'

'It's all right for you, Cass, but I have to live with these people, we have to get on together. *You* still have a life outside these four walls. I don't!'

'Oh yeah, my life's so great, isn't it? A mountain of student debt; a mortgage that was supposed to be shared with my dear ex-husband; a succession of crappy jobs going nowhere.'

'I don't know why you married him. You always said you wouldn't marry an actor; they were too narcissistic. He was a real piece of work. It really upset Mum and Dad.'

'It seemed like a good idea at the time. In retrospect, the only good thing I got from that marriage was a move up the alphabet, from 'Pratt' to 'Green' in one go.'

Cass was relieved to see Alison smile. She went back into the kitchen to put on the kettle. Alison followed and began loading the dishwasher. 'Want a cuppa?' Cass asked, but her sister said no, she was afloat with tea after that Neighbourhood Watch meeting,

'How did you get on with Dr O'Neil?' Alison asked. 'I was surprised you got around to phoning him so soon.'

'Oh, OK,' Cass said, but she didn't mention the nightmares that had prompted her to make that early morning call. She'd woken in a cold sweat at 5 a.m. from a dream that left her shaking. She'd dreamed that she'd been eating herself, as her hands and feet turned into the paws of an animal she gnawed on her own bones. This was becoming a recurrent nocturnal horror, each time more vivid and repulsive.

'Did you tell him about the wolf?' asked Alison.

'No, it was just a five-minute thing, not a proper consultation. But I'm seeing him this Wednesday lunchtime – I don't suppose coming over here would be possible?'

'Don't even think it! Wednesday afternoon is my turn to hold a play date here for three of Debbie's little friends from Toddler Group.'

'Oh, I'll find somewhere else, no problem. By the way, I've

met him before, you know?'

'Really?' There was a slight frown that vanished almost at once as Alison turned away to load the last cup into the dishwasher.

'Yes, I bumped into him in the bookshop the other day. I knew he seemed familiar. Couldn't place him at first.'

'Oh, well, that would be it,' said Alison with a shrug. 'Right, I'm going to collect Debbie from her playdate with Trudy's kids, then nipping down the shops before school run time.' And she headed for the door, leaving Cass to nurse a mug of tea and wonder if that nice-looking Dr O'Neil – Declan – was single? He wasn't wearing a wedding ring for sure. She brushed the thought away with an involuntary wave of her hand. This was to be a purely professional relationship.

*

The flat was hardly ideal for a consultation given the state of the place, but after Alison's unreasonable refusal to host the session there was no real alternative. Cass only hoped that the corner of her lounge where she had placed a chair by the sofa would do for now. Weren't you supposed to lie down on a sofa to unburden yourself to a shrink? Or was that just in old movies? At least it would be private here as Barycz and young Andy his apprentice had gone on a long lunch break, assuring her they'd be back in a tick. So everything was ready for Declan O'Neil. He at least arrived promptly, with a notebook in hand. Old school, thought Cass, pre-digital. Or maybe it was just to keep things off the record where the tax man was concerned? It did cross her mind.

'I hope this isn't too basic?' she said apologetically, showing him to the chair with a carefully placed cushion covering the paint stain on its seat.

'It's fine. So, if you make yourself comfortable. Let's run through – no you don't have to lie down, let's just sit and chat. This is a fairly informal session.'

'Oh, OK,' said Cass. Having draped herself over the sofa, she sat up smartly swinging her legs round just as he was sitting down, clipping him on the shins with her foot. Awkward.

'Sorry!'

'Sorry!'

He opened his notebook and they ran through a few preliminaries as Cass tried to suppress her embarrassment. She was happy enough to talk about general issues, skirting around anything too specific, and was just beginning to feel a little more at ease – and that was when the drilling started. Loud, persistent drilling. The whole room seemed to be vibrating with the sound. Cass turned and banged hard on the wall behind her. The drilling stopped for a moment and young Andy's head appeared in the doorway looking blank. His usual expression to be fair.

'Andy, I thought you chaps had gone out for lunch?' said Cass.

'Yeah, well, we were – and now we're back, Mr Barycz says we've got to crack on if we're gonna be finished on time.'

'Can't you pause it for an hour? I have a meeting going on here?'

There was a sharp intake of breath from Andy. 'I'll go an'

ask him, and see what he says, but he won't like it.' He disappeared back through the doorway. A moment's pause them the drilling started up again. Clearly Mr Barycz had spoken.

Declan sighed and looked at his watch. 'Perhaps we could reschedule for another day?' He was already half rising to leave. This was a man who had little time to waste.

'No! I mean, we're doing so well, why don't we take it outside?'

'What?'

'A walk? Let's walk and talk – down by the river?'

'The river? It's been a long time…' his face softened and there was an almost wistful look in his eyes. He had nice eyes, she'd noticed that when she first saw him in the bookshop. 'It's not far,' said Cass, 'Come on, let's go!'

*

So it was that they found themselves walking along beside the green-grey Thames, down by the Cutty Sark floating on its billow of glass waves that glinted in the sunlight. Cass had been coming down here since childhood to visit the old wooden tea clipper docked here after its life at sea. As a few clouds glided over the sun the glass surround became transparent and you could glimpse the tourists down below walking the length of the ship's iron hull. There was a cluster of ship's figureheads down there, though it would cost you to go inside for a closer look. It was windy today, though the weather had been sunny earlier in the week, and Cass pulled an old waxed fishing hat over her hair. It did the job, even if it wasn't a fashion statement.

'I didn't think it would be quite so bracing,' she apologised.

'No, it's great to be out in the open air for a change,' said Declan. 'I should do all my consultations like this from now on! Don't you love the river Thames?'

'Yes, I suppose so. I'm a Londoner born and bred, so I must love it, it's my river.' Actually, her childhood river had been a sad little tributary of the mighty Thames called the Quaggy, a trickle of dirty water commonly used for fly tipping, where they'd gone to catch tiddlers as kids. These days she understood it had been cleaned up and undergone gentrification at the hands of The Friends of the Quaggy.

'So full of history,' Declan said, 'down that way is Wapping where they used to hang pirates and smugglers "the washing of three tides". I had a friend who was a Blue Badge Guide, used to walk me off my feet and tell me all the old stories of London. But we're not here to talk about me.'

'No, well, it's difficult....' She squashed her hat more firmly onto her head and paused.

'Trust me, I'm a psychiatrist – I've heard it all before. People feel unhappy, dissatisfied, even angry about their lives–'

'Isn't that what they call the human condition?'

'True. But when you came to the office you mentioned anger management issues?'

'Yes,' Cass said. 'But I don't want pills.'

'I agree, although in some cases they are beneficial, drugs

aren't always the answer. For instance, sometimes, we have women coming to us feeling more or less invisible, lacking in confidence, and one of the spin-offs of working for the NHS is that we can offer therapeutic breast enhancement.'

'What? You think I need a boob job?' asked Cass, cutting in before he could offer her any manner of nip, tuck or enhancement. She began to giggle in spite of herself.

'No, no, not at all – I've never prescribed that kind of treatment myself – I was merely saying there are alternatives to medication, and that just happens to be one of them. Bad example! There are other therapeutic treatments like tattoo removal.'

Cass took pity on his embarrassment and put on her serious face. 'I did go for a tattoo once when I was feeling rebellious but chickened out and had my ears pierced instead.'

'How did that work out for you?'

'Not great,' she said and pulled back her hair from the left side. A missing earlobe told its own story.

'Oh, I hadn't noticed,' said Declan.

'It doesn't bother me.' She tipped back her head and shook her hair back into place. A sudden gust of wind took the opportunity to whip her hat away, and send it spinning towards the water. Declan made a grab for it, but it was over the edge of the railing too soon for him to catch.

'Careful!' Cass grabbed his arm. 'It's only an old filming hat.'

'It's OK,' he smiled.' I'm a strong swimmer; but not a total idiot. I'm afraid that's one old hat away down the river.'

Cass smiled back at him and let go of his arm. Talking a riverside walk had been a good move. This felt more relaxed and natural, even if it was beginning to cloud over. She found herself opening up a little about the annoyances of her working life. Only the stuff that was safe to talk about, of course.

'Honestly by now I thought I'd be further on with my career, not stuck in the same old rut of shitty jobs and trying to stay pleasant with people who haven't half a brain – sorry, but it makes me angry. Really pisses me off!'

'Isn't that what someone once called the human condition?' he said, with gentle amusement in his blue-grey eyes.

'Very funny,' said Cass, 'but you don't know what it's like, always running as fast as you can just to stay in the same place, like the Red Queen in *Alice Through the Looking Glass*.'

'Don't I? You'd be surprised. But tell me about this anger of yours – what kind of manifestation does it take?'

'Manifestation?' Cass repeated uneasily. Oh no, it was far too soon to be telling him about her dream-wolf. She didn't want him to think she was crazy, did she?

'Um, the usual way,' she said, 'I get a wee bit sarcastic, then I have to bite my tongue and try not say anything too outrageous. I don't shout and throw things if that's what you were thinking. You have to bottle it up, don't you? You can't go around getting mad at people, can you? In my line of work, you have to be *nice* to people. Even if they are dickheads. Sometimes I feel I'll never make anything of my life – I'll end up as one of those old ladies who live in two rooms with a cat and buy all their clothes from charity shops.'

'This jacket came from a charity shop,' said Declan wryly, 'I thought it was a real bargain. Dry cleaned and all.'

'It's a very nice pre-loved garment,' said Cass. It was a smart-casual lightweight grey linen that had probably enjoyed an upmarket earlier life with a previous owner before slipping out of favour.

'Pre-loved? Is that what they call it now? I'll have to remember that,' he said.

'Well, I'm sorry this consultation hasn't gone quite to plan, but I want to reassure you that nothing you've told me so far seems life-threatening. And as for anger management, I can recommend a book on mindfulness and you can self-refer to Healthy Minds who do some excellent counselling work by phone.'

'But don't we have another session together?' asked Cass quickly. 'Isn't it *buy one get one free?*'

'It's fifty pounds for the first two consultations, thirty per session after that' he said, 'If you feel it would be of benefit, we could meet again. I'd have to check my diary back at the office.'

'Yes, please. I'm free anytime. My next job doesn't start for a while. Oh, and I was wondering: why did you say you were a strong swimmer?'

'Oh, I used to do a lot of wild swimming at one time. But I wasn't going to jump in after your hat! Your hair looks good without it.' Cass felt a little wriggle of pleasure at the compliment.

'I've swum in Fiji, Norway, the Caribbean,' he went on, 'I preferred the Caribbean, though the icy cold water in the Norwegian fjords does make you feel you're alive. Your heart's pumping, and your energy comes from your emotions – like anger, fear or love – keeping you going when you think you can't.'

'I didn't take you for an outdoor type. Being a psychiatrist?'

'Huh! Not anymore. I'm really out of condition.' He patted his midriff with one hand, though there was not too much of a belly, as far as Cass could tell. He looked in pretty good shape to her for a man of thirty-nine, forty?

A few fat drops of rain splashed onto her face.

'Ah, petrichor,' said Declan. 'Can't you smell it? That smell that always comes with the first rain after a dry spell?'

'I didn't know it had a name.'

'It didn't till a couple of Australian scientists invented one back in the 1960s, I think it was. *Petrus* – Latin for stone , and *ichor* – the blood of the gods. Useful word for pub quizzes.'

'Does something always have to have a name to exist? Why can't it just be *that smell?*'

'Questions of existential phenomenology are a bit above my pay grade.'

'Now you're just saying words!'

'Maybe so,' he grinned, 'But we humans need to give things a name. It's hard wired into us. And isn't it the nameless fears that are always the worst? The ones we're afraid to name?' He gave her a sideways glance as they walked on through the light summer shower that flecked his jacket with rain droplets. Cass said nothing.

'We have five minutes left, if you don't mind walking to the car park with me? Don't mind a bit of rain?'

'Of course,' said Cass and shadowed him along Church Street.

'Was there anything else you wanted to discuss?' asked Declan casually.

'Not that I can think of for the moment,' Cass lied. Of course, there was a whole lot more, they both knew it; but that was for another day.

When they reached the car park, Declan shook her hand in a rather formal gesture and said goodbye, that he would text her the date of their next appointment, and how enjoyable it had been to get out of the hospital for an hour. Then he climbed into a large, rather battered yellow bus, with a faded logo on the side that read 'Sunshine Day Centre', leaving Cass to wonder if he was moonlighting as a bus driver as well as running these cash-in-hand consultations on the side. Oh God, she'd forgotten to pay him! Oh well, there'd be a next time. And maybe a time after that?

Chapter 11

Thursday

On Thursday morning Cass put an empty rucksack on her back and took a bus down to Greenwich. Sometime soon she'd get around to fixing that puncture but for the moment her bike was out of action. She needed some fresh clothes and more than that she needed to check up on the builders.

The skip resting outside her flat looked suspiciously full of stuff that had never seen the inside of her home – but that was the way of skips. Neighbours passing by might just as well help themselves to some unwanted item as dump some of their own rubbish there. It was a kind of urban yin and yang arrangement. She herself had found an old Victorian mirror in a skip and once cleaned up it had become quite presentable.

Cass opened her front door and coughed on the miasma of brick dust and God knows what else in the tiny hallway. She squeezed past a couple of trestles that were taking up most of the space. 'Mr Barycz? Andy? Are you there?' she called hopefully. No reply, but somewhere beyond a radio was playing.

The lounge door was slightly ajar. 'Lounge' being a posh

word for the room that doubled as lounge, dining room and kitchen, though there was a door to shut off the tiny kitchen area where the ceiling had come down forcing her to take refuge with Alison, closely followed by the leak from the *bedroom* ceiling precipitating that unfortunate incident in the laundrette. Cass pushed open the door and stood for a moment observing two workmen standing in the middle of the room watching a slow drip from the lounge ceiling land in a bucket carefully placed beneath it.

'Mr Barycz,' she said very calmly, 'what is that bucket doing there?'

Barycz and Andy jumped and turned round.

'Mrs Green, I didn't hear you come in,' said Barycz. He was a stocky little man with a hopeful comb-over hairstyle that really did not convince.

'I thought you'd fixed the leaky pipework?'

'Oh yes, the kitchen and bedroom's all done now, you take a look. But this morning we have a new drip,' he shrugged and spread his hands in a plumber's gesture of mild despair. 'It's an old heating system – the pipes are under too much pressure – a two-minute job once I fit the new pump. But it's an old model, I had to order it specially.'

'Oh, well,' said Cass, 'let's get on with it.'

But Mr Barycz would not be hurried when he had a story to tell. 'So I went to my friend Stanley's shop to pick it up this morning – and there it is, sitting on the counter waiting for me – your new pump. But the shop's all closed up – gone into receivership. A sign on the door and everything.'

Andy shook his head in mute disbelief, though he must have heard the whole sad tale before. Possibly more than once.

'Can't you break in and get it?' said Cass, drawing a sharp intake of breath from Barycz and more head shaking from Andy.

'Don't worry, Mrs Green, we've turned off the water at the mains. And I know a supplier in Camberwell who can do me another pump by this afternoon, if you can pay for it? It will all be fixed by tomorrow.'

'You've been saying that for six weeks,' said Cass, beginning to feel that she was losing the will to live. 'Just make sure it is, please. Text me and let me know how much. I'll transfer the money for the pump when you've got it.'

She went off to her bedroom to collect a few clothes, stuffing them into her rucksack in a hurry. Her hand hesitated over a little black dress that has once been a favourite but now bearing a dribble of wine stains from some long-forgotten party. A pity, but this one was for the charity shop or recycling. She pulled it out of the wardrobe and tucked it into the top of her rucksack, then she was good to go.

*

Cass got off the bus at the bottom of Blackheath village and began to walk up past the shops. She was about to donate her little black dress into one of the charity shops when she realised that the display of garments in the window were all in better nick than her party frock. She felt ashamed, it surely wasn't fair to give them her old tat and expect them to clean it and sell it? Then she was struck by the thought that it might yet be salvageable in that dry-cleaners that did a Gold Service? Might be worth a try.

There was a small Asian woman wearing a smart blue checked overall at the desk, who cast a professional eye over Cass's dress.

'It's probably past it,' said Cass apologetically, ready to whisk it away.

'Wine stains?'

'Yes, I'm afraid so. I won't waste your time.' Cass put out a hand to remove the garment.

'No, no, no,' said the lady, patting Cass's hand, 'you leave this with me. Gold Service? We can have it ready for you next week. It will be fine, you'll see. What's your name, please, and phone number?' She was already writing out a green ticket as Cass gave her contact details.

Cass was glad to think that the dress might well be wearable again, it had always looked good on her. Then she immediately felt guilty about *not* donating it to the charity shop after all and put a couple of pound coins in the local Hospice Box on the counter.

'Goodbye! God bless you,' said the lady, as Cass turned to leave.

On her walk back to Alison's Cass remembered how, as a child, she'd been brought up to call all unknowns by the polite 'lady' or 'gentleman', whilst adult friends of her parents would be 'Aunty' or 'Uncle'. Was it a south east London thing, a working-class thing, or something handed down in the family? No one was called a 'lady' now, unless in a postmodern ironic way. Even that Dimbleby bloke on that TV programme her Dad used to watch had stopped using it to call out members of the audience to give their questions. Everyone was a woman or a man now. Was that Dimbleby bloke still doing that show? Probably not, and Dad had passed away more than ten years ago, so no use asking him without the use of a Ouija board. It certainly wasn't the kind of TV her Mum watched, though she could probably catch you up with *Neighbours*, her daytime drug of choice.

*

When Cass opened the front door, she found Alison carrying Debbie up the stairs.

'Go and put the coffee on, 'said Allie, 'I'll be with you in a minute.'

'Has Debbie hurt herself?' asked Cass.

'No, but she wants me to carry her up and down for the moment.'

Debbie's little face peered down at Cass over her mum's shoulder. 'I don't like that man with horns on the stairs,' she said in a low voice, then hid her face away.

Cass was puzzled but went into the kitchen and made a cafetière of Colombian. Alison joined her in a few moments.

'So what's all this about?' asked Cass.

'Something's spooked Debbie, so she won't go up and down on her own. She's probably seen something scary on TV, or in a picture book – I don't know. It will pass.'

Alison's children were not allowed smartphones or tablets

till they were older, so it wouldn't be that, as Cass knew. But still she wondered. 'You don't think she did see something? Staircases are often haunted – remember the Tulip staircase in the Queen's House? That photo of a hooded figure?'

'Don't be ridiculous. Oh, for heaven's sake, Cass, you don't still believe in all that ghost stuff? It's imagination, it's what children do – they scare themselves silly, then it's all forgotten in a while.'

'You still think my wolf *tulpa* is imaginary, don't you?'

'I'm not getting into that – you have a therapist to deal with it now,' said Alison firmly. 'Anyway, what was it about the Queen's House? I vaguely remember going there on a school trip?'

'So did we, when I was eleven. It was pretty boring – rooms full of paintings of old white men in wigs, as my BFF Keisha said. I wonder what happened to Keisha? Anyway, the only good bit was the Tulip Staircase which was supposed to be haunted. Back in the sixties some Canadian tourist took a photo of a couple of ghostly figures on the stairs. We all started running up and down making spooky noises and got told off by the curator. Miss Withers was mortified – she never had any control over us, poor thing. I wonder whatever happened to Miss Withers?'

'I can show you,' said Alison, picking up her phone and doing a quick search. The picture of a stern looking woman in a navy-blue jacket appeared. 'Look – she went into politics, joined the Conservative Party and is MP for Bexley or somewhere.'

'Gosh! She looks like she toughened up after she left teaching.'

'I expect it was your lot that toughened her up. Parliament would be a doddle after Year Seven school outings.'

'Dad always said *you* should go into politics – what else would you do with a First in PPE?' said Cass. 'Dad thought you should be running the country – or become a "Lady Bishop".'

'I don't think so,' Alison smiled. 'Anyway, I liked teaching mathematics. I could always go back. They're crying out for maths teachers, offering golden handshakes. Or try something completely different? I could become a professional Cupcake Baker to the Stars – I've had enough practice making cakes for school fetes.'

'Your cupcakes are legendary. You could go on Bake Off!'

'Thank you, dear sister. But just getting through one day at a time will do me for now. You will be here for dinner tomorrow evening, won't you? It's the one night that Ted promises to be home, I feed the children early tea and get them settled down, then we have a lovely, calm, civilised dinner together. It's my one little haven of peace I look forward to all week. And Friday night is pie night. Don't be late.'

'OK. Speaking of food, I haven't had any lunch – is there anything going?'

'There's some left-over quiche and salad in the fridge.'

'Thanks.' Cass went to help herself to whatever was available. 'Then I'll nip down to that little nail bar in the parade – my nails need some serious repair work – maybe they can do a pedicure while I'm there. What? Don't give me that look. Oh don't worry I'll take my rucksack up to my room before I leave.'

'It's not that – just I wish I could nip down to a nail bar whenever I felt like it!'

*

Later as Alison watched her sister go trotting off down the road a funny old rhyme Dad used to tell them popped into her head:

Last night I saw upon the stair
A little man who was not there
He wasn't there again today
Oh how I wish he'd go away.

She closed the front door and went back inside to run a quick load of washing before Debbie woke from her nap and they'd have to go and pick up the twins from school. As she loaded the Bosch washing machine (technology you could trust) Alison wondered how many people saw things that weren't there? Recently someone on her Mum's Group had posted a query: *Has anyone else with a toddler noticed anything weird? When I took mine to the park he pointed out the little boy playing with a ball beneath the bridge – but when I looked there was no one there.* Maybe children could see things they didn't yet know they weren't supposed to see? And she remembered Dad complaining about those annoying 'little black men' running around the room until he recovered from his stroke and began to act normal again. What did he see? Kobolds? Brownies? Gnomes or sprites? Or merely the products of his temporarily befuddled brain – much like her sister's imaginary wolf friend.

She knew that Ted made a very good living out of persuading clients not to see things they really oughtn't to see. His Harley Street practice attracted the occasional *Hello* celeb, a couple of politicians from either side of the House, and even the odd minor Royal with an embarrassing problem, though of course he was far too discreet to discuss any of this with her. Right, the wash was on, just time to prep a few bits for dinner before the school run.

*

It wasn't until later that night as she snuggled in bed, warming her cold feet on Ted's solid calves, that Alison's mind began to wander again. Ted was already asleep, nothing would wake him till morning, not police sirens, children crying, nor an owl's ghostly snoring outside their window. The first time she had heard that particular sound was when Ted was away at a conference and she was alone at night. It had freaked her out – it really did sound like the ghost of an old man snoring right by her bedroom window. But when she Googled it, Alison discovered it was the call of a young barn owl. It must have lost its way in leafy Blackheath and settled by her window. A ghostly snoring becomes a snoring ghost – why do we do it? Why turn the perfectly normal into the paranormal?

Then she remembered something she'd heard on one of those American TV cop shows her mother used to watch constantly – CSI or NCIS – when that silver fox guy her mother was so keen on – Grissom or Gibbs? – said something about us being hardwired to believe in the supernatural from earliest times? Back in the days when our ancestors trekked the savannahs and saw the breeze rustling the long grasses they imagined it was a lion lurking there. An instinct for survival. It might be a real lion – or a real ghost – best not to take any chances or you might go extinct. And wasn't there an article in *New Scientist* (when she still had half a brain and time to read) that said much the same thing? And then there was that feminist writer on the radio who said that ghosts and apparitions were merely ways for women to express feelings and experiences that were socially unacceptable in the patriarchy…

She yawned and turned on her left side, back to back with Ted, a warm, dependable presence, then a half forgotten memory came to mind of another warm body beside her after a long day by the sea in Spain, their one holiday together, and how sweet the smell of his sweat in the darkness, as if the salt of the ancient ocean was tangled in his hair… She pushed that image away, after all it wasn't as if he was always in her mind, was it? But as she drifted off, a fragment of that old rhyme popped into her head again:

He wasn't there again today
Oh how I wish he'd go away.

Chapter 12

Hot Summer Night

Alison was drawing breath and drinking a large glass of Pino Grigio at the kitchen table. Everything was OK. Everything would be all right. This was her mantra for tonight; the steak and kidney pie was in the oven, the organic veg prepared for steaming, the dessert made and sitting in the fridge. The children had eaten their tea without too many fights over 'nasty courgette basgetti' – which was *not at all* nasty and *very good* for them (though sometimes she herself longed for the tinned spaghetti on toast of her own childhood: full of salt, sugar and carbs, sprinkled with fast melting grated Cheddar and tasting like heaven). And for once Ted was home early on a Friday night to read them a bedtime story 'with all the voices'. And Cass was sitting in the lounge studying a book on mindfulness and had not said anything too mad for quite a while. Alison loved her little sister dearly, but there were times when her weird piques and fancies were a bit much. There was that time she'd filled the kitchen cupboard with jars of pink Himalayan rock salt steeped in water that was supposed to do something amazing for you, or the time she'd gone on a green tea diet and nearly killed herself – OK, that was back in her teenage years, when everyone was allowed to go a bit crazy. But this latest fantasy was a bit hard to take, so it was a relief to see that she seemed to have calmed down a bit. Sending her to Ted's best friend – let's be honest, his only friend – had obviously had some beneficial effect, even though Cass admitted she still hadn't come clean about the wolf thing. The doorbell rang and broke into Alison's stream of consciousness.

'OK, I'll get it,' called Cass from the lounge, as Alison was getting up from the kitchen table and her empty glass.

Alison followed Cass down the hall in time to see her open the front door and pause. Outside on the doorstep stood Declan O'Neil holding two bottles – one red, one white. No one said anything for a moment. *Oh shit!* thought Alison. This is going to be awkward.

*

The steak and kidney pie along with mountains of mashed potatoes was going down a treat, and Ted, after three glasses of red, was holding forth on some of the terribly amusing things they'd got up to in their old student days. Alison was still fuming with him for bringing home Declan without forewarning her, but Cass and Declan were being the perfect guests, hardly saying a thing over dinner. Alison could only guess at how they must be feeling.

'So, Dec tells me not to worry, he'll climb up the drainpipe and in through the window then come down and let me in – we were both bladdered, but it's a good thing one of us had a head for heights in those days. Do you remember, Allie?

You'd locked yourself out of the flat?' said Ted.

'It was a long time ago,' Alison said.

'I didn't realise you'd all been such good friends back at Uni,' said Cass, with a glance at her sister.

'More pie anyone?' was all Alison could reply.

'We used to go to that pub – the Old Blue Cheese?' said Ted. 'Did you frequent the Old Blue Cheese in your day, Cass?'

'I wasn't Oxbridge material like you clever chaps; I went to Hull, remember?'

'Oh, yes. Very cold up there.'

'Yes, it was positively Siberian in the Autumn term – and most of the Spring term,' Cass said. 'No punting on the river for us. No May Day Ball.'

'Ready for dessert?' Alison quickly cleared away the plates and headed for the kitchen. So far so good. Just keep them eating and hope that no one said anything that might make Ted suspicious. Of what? Well, anything going on behind his back. Cass and Declan could keep their arrangement secret. At that point Ted came into the kitchen with an empty wine bottle, looking for a replacement.

'Haven't you had enough to drink?' said Alison sharply, taking the empty bottle and dropping it into the recycling bin.

'I don't know what's up with you this evening,' he said reproachfully, 'You've been badgering me to bring Declan home for dinner for ages, and now you go all funny on me. Hey, wouldn't it be a laugh if he made a play for your little sister?'

'Oh, shut up, Ted!'

'What? I thought you wanted to fix him up with one of your girlfriends? Why not Cass? She's at a loose end, not bad looking?'

'Oh, try to make yourself useful, take the dessert in for me,' Alison said, pushing a large bowl of tiramisu into hands. She shoved him out of the door and picked up a tray of handmade stoneware dishes to carry through to the dining table where Cass and Declan had been left by themselves too long for comfort in her opinion.

Back at the table Ted replenished glasses as Alison served the tiramisu.

'God, we had some wild old times back in the day,' Ted began, but Alison cut him short with a warning look.

'So, what's your take on this Deptford Wolf story?' she asked Declan, steering the conversation away from any more student reminiscences that might be dredged up. 'Do you have some clever theory?'

'Ah, don't get him started on all that old wolfman business,' Ted groaned. 'Cass doesn't want to know about Declan's obsession with all that guff – do you?'

Cass merely smiled and shrugged her shoulders in a non-committal way, while Declan looked embarrassed.

'But I'm interested,' said Alison. 'Have the papers got it right? Does he transform into a wolf every full moon?'

'Of course not, 'said Declan. 'but that doesn't mean to say that animal passion isn't at the root of his condition.'

'Condition?' said Alison. 'I'd call it a bit more than a

condition: He goes out murdering innocent women. He leaves a red rose by the corpse.'

'How did you know that?' asked Ted through a mouthful of cream.

'Don't you ever follow the news? said Alison. 'Go on Dec, what's the red rose thing all about?'

'Traditionally a single blood red rose is a symbol of true love; but in this case it might be 'if I can't have her, nobody can'. But I don't think so; I think he's in love with death. I think maybe that's what the single red rose means? Not Eros but Thanatos? Death itself?'

'Really? And what would you think if he'd left a lupin or a petunia?' asked Ted, with another spoonful of tiramisu half way to his mouth.

'Oh, you're impossible!' said Alison and started clearing away the dessert bowls almost before he'd finished eating his seconds. 'You two infinitely stupid male creatures!' (Although a quote from Shaw's *Pygmalion* would be lost on them, she couldn't resist dropping it in.) 'The red rose is nothing to do with any of that: don't you get it? I've just remembered, Ted, back at Uni you gave me a single red rose. It was very romantic. Only you didn't bring it over to the flat yourself – it was a delivery man with a motorbike or a van – and I opened the door to him? Oh God, don't you see? *That's* how the killer gains access to his victims. They open their door to him.'

'I never sent you a single red rose,' said Ted, holding on to his dessert dish and helping himself to another quick dollop of tiramisu and cream. There was a moment's silence broken only by the sound of a spoon scraping against stoneware that set your teeth on edge.

'That would have been me,' said Declan quietly.

Cass looked at him, then across the dinner table at her sister. And Alison could see a light bulb go on in her sister's mind. Oh, bollocks!

'Let me help you with the dishes, Allie?' and Cass was on her feet before Alison could stop her.

Once in the kitchen, Cass cornered her: 'It's Dexy, isn't it? Why didn't you tell me Dr Declan O'Neil was Dexy? You broke his heart.'

'Oh, that's rubbish,' Alison protested.

'Mum said you did.'

'How would she know? We only went out for a few months when we were both Freshers. That was years and years ago; I didn't think you'd remember him.'

'Why wouldn't I remember him? All the boys in my GCSE year were spotty faced loons and Dexy was the most gorgeous thing to ever walk through our front door! He came to stay with us – twice – it's all come back to me now. Then you gave him the push and started going out with *Call-me-Ted.*'

'Why did you always call him that behind his back?'

'Because that's who he was – *Call-me-Ted* – not even his real name, is it?'

'Would you want to be called *Theodore?* Oh, for heaven's sake go and make polite conversation with Declan and send Ted out here to help me load the dishwasher. Apparently only men know how to load a dishwasher correctly.'

'*Dexy* – you should have told me, Allie,' said Cass, pausing in the doorway. 'God, it's almost incestuous.'

'Scoot!' said Alison, throwing a tea towel at her annoying little sister.

*

The rest of the evening passed quickly with decaff coffee and a few chocolates left over from someone's birthday. But Cass watched her sister with a new eye. Alison was better at keeping secrets than she remembered. Clearly, she'd learned a poker face somewhere along the way from childhood to motherhood. Must be useful when married to a psychiatrist, thought Cass, if not essential. There would always be things better for Ted not to know.

When the time came for Declan to leave, it was Cass who fetched his coat and walked with him to the door. Standing on the doorstep they had a few moments to talk unobserved. It had been a case of walking on eggshells all evening, but they'd pulled it off.

'Ted has no idea about our arrangement, has he?' Declan asked.

'No! Alison gave me your number. I'll understand if you want me to find another therapist.'

'Why? Because your sister and I used to be an item back in the day? Or is it because of Ted? You know that anything you tell me is in confidence.'

'No, not if it doesn't bother you. And I'd still like to have that second consultation?'

'OK, but I'm afraid it will have to be at my office – I'm on a very tight schedule next week. We'll have to sneak you in past Marge.'

'Thanks. You know, I can remember times you came to stay with us?'

'I'm not sure I recall meeting you then – there was a little sister; but I'm pretty sure she didn't have red hair. Was there another one of you girls?'

'No, that was *me* in my Goth phase. Black hair, black dress, Doc Martin boots?'

'So that was you, was it? The little Goth girl who followed us around.'

'Not *that* little, I was almost fifteen. I felt quite grown up at the time, thank you,' said Cass, who sometimes felt that she was still that little Goth girl on the inside who'd never quite grown up. Declan said goodbye and she watched him walk down the road and around the corner to where she guessed he had left the Fun Bus, having tactfully avoided parking outside Ted and Alison's house. What a lovely man she thought, all these years and still the most gorgeous thing to walk through the door. What a pity this was doomed to be a purely professional relationship.

Chapter 13

The Bechdel Test

Tidying up the kitchen later that night both sisters avoided any mention of what had gone before other than Alison's brief 'You Ok then?' and Cass's equally brief 'All good.'

The last of the cutlery had gone into the dishwasher and the last *handwash only* glass had been carefully laid to rest on a superabsorbent cloth on the draining board before Alison asked casually how well things were going in therapy?

'Fine, like I told you. Early days yet, but talking's good, isn't it?' Cass said.

'Yes, I believe so – though sometimes you might need more help to get to grips with things…'

'What are you getting at? Oh for God's sake, Allie, you don't think I'm doing drugs? Come on! You know me better than that.'

'I know, but – well, you never know with some people. Things can seem quite normal then suddenly they go all weird as hell – do you remember my old school friend Sarah Chalmers-Smith?'

'Vaguely – you were so far above me that we hardly mixed.'

'We did mix – at Founders' Day and Sports Day and Drama Club.'

Cass did not recall school days with any great affection, never got to be a prefect, unlike Alison, who had even been in the running for Head Girl at one time. Their school was a glossy new comprehensive that came trailing clouds of glory from the direct grant selective girls' grammar school it had originally been on its previous high street site. By the time Cass joined the school boys had also been admitted and the whole place had gone to pot in the estimation of former alumni. However it did still boast some beautiful stained glass windows transported from the old building and a School Anthem that, once learned never forgotten, would be sung in rousing drunken chorus at later reunions.

'Yes, so what about Sarah double-barrelled?'

'Well, she had a problem a bit like yours.'

'Really?'

'Yes. Vampires.'

'What?'

'She was attacked by vampires in Eastern Europe – can't remember exactly where.'

Cass sat down, grabbed a glass and helped herself to the last trickle of wine from a bottle on the table. This was too good to be missed. 'Spill! All the gory details.'

'Ok, so about a year ago – it was after her second divorce – Sarah went a bit New Age and bought herself a big camper van thing, like a Winnebago, and set herself up in a vintage clothing business, buying and selling and travelling. Really suited her too. Anyway, she was travelling through – oh, I don't know where...'

'Transylvania?'

'Very funny, no, Bulgaria or somewhere like that, and she began to have these horrible nightmares about something heavy pressing down on her chest and having visions of thin, pale people looking in through the windows at her as she slept… Vampires.'

'Really? Really, truly vampires?

'No, of course not. It was like one of those Fred Vargas detective novels you gave me to read – werewolves and vampire killers that always turned out to be Scooby Doos?'

'You mean it was the school janitor in a mask all the time?'

'Exactly.'

'So what about Sarah's vampires?'

'When she got back to England she went to her GP and was expecting to be sent off to the Funny Farm – I'm sorry, I shouldn't have said that. It was inappropriate – '

'Never mind. Go on.'

'They sent her for some blood tests at a tropical hygiene hospital, or wherever it was. And it turns out she'd caught some rare virus that you only get in the Balkans that gives you these bizarre hypnogogic hallucinations, that's what they called it, coupled with breathlessness – hence: vampires!'

'Scooby Doo!

'Scooby Scooby Doo.' Alison nodded.

'And you think that's what's wrong with me? Some rare Balkan virus? I've never been anywhere remotely near the

Balkans – I'm not sure I could even point them out on a map.'

'Don't be silly. I only meant that there is always a scientific explanation for this kind of stuff – even if we don't know it yet. And I can't think of anyone less imaginative than Sarah whatever her surname is now, so she wasn't making any of this up. She really did believe it at the time.'

'Wasn't she captain of school hockey?'

'Exactly. She was terrifyingly good too. Anyway, all I'm saying is everything is going to be OK. Bedtime.'

'Bedtime,' Cass agreed and washed up her wineglass at the kitchen tap, which was, of course one of those posh ones that dispenses boiling water or chilled water, or whatever else your heart might desire, and which she could not afford to install in her own humble abode. Wickes or Homebase would do just fine for her.

*

Once in bed Cass fell asleep almost immediately. Only the faint ticking of two or three long case clocks downstairs, some of Ted's antique investments, with their out of sync chiming throughout the night might be expected to wake her from her rest. Why Ted couldn't manage to get those wretched clocks to chime in musical accord on the hour and the quarters, rather than randomly, had always puzzled Cass, but she was getting used to it now. It did not seem to bother anyone else; they *must* be used to it by now.

But it wasn't an errant clock chiming that woke her – it was the landing light spilling into her room from the door opening. A small figure stood in the doorway. Cass sat up in bed.

'What's the matter Debs? Bad dream?'

Debbie nodded her head and came running over to the bedside. Cass reached out and gathered her up in her arms. She smelled of warm, slightly wet night-time nappy and baby shampoo. Cass would not have called herself a maternal person, but there was something appealing about this little niece of hers. She gave her a hug.

'Come on, let's get you back to bed. I'll sit with you for a while, OK?'

Debbie nodded, one finger in her mouth, as Cass swung herself out of bed and hoisted the child onto her hip. Debbie clung there like a monkey, wrapping her arms and legs around her, as Cass carried her over to the door.

Once out onto the landing they were only a few steps away from the child's bedroom when something came sliding up the stairs like a grey mist, growing more and more solid as it bounded towards them. Cass took a step backwards, trying to get the bedroom door between them and it, but the wolf launched itself towards her and snatched the child from her arms. Debbie howled louder than any wolf as it shook her and threw her aside, then came at Cass, burying its teeth deep into her thigh. The pain was sharp, piercing and very real.

'No! You can't do that to *me* – this is *my* dream!' Cass screamed in surprise and disbelief.

She woke herself up shouting 'No!' so loudly that she hoped no one else had heard her cry out. No wolf, no child of course – just a throbbing pain in her leg that slowly faded as she rubbed it. She could almost feel the indentations of teeth in her flesh – but that was plain ridiculous. Dreams don't leave scars, do they? But maybe Alison was right, perhaps her wolf was some kind of waking nightmare. How bad could that be? Certainly not as bad as some rare Balkan virus that opened the door to vampire attacks. Come to think of it she pitied any vampire that went up against Sarah double-barrelled armed with her hockey stick. Sarah had once broken a girl's thumb in a bully-off and given another poor girl a nosebleed whilst committing the sin of 'sticks' in an inter-year match. And that other girl had been Cass on both occasions, as she recalled.

No, she would be fine until the next session with Declan gave her a chance to talk this through properly. Next time she would summon up the courage to tell him the whole sorry saga and they would reason it out and put it away forever. Meanwhile she had a couple of days to keep an eye on her flat and go to choose her new fitted kitchen units in whatever perpetual sale was on. Real life, normal life would be her salvation. And if only those bloody clocks would stop chiming the quarters in discord maybe she could get a decent night's sleep after all.

Chapter 14

Procrastination

Declan was full of good intentions that Saturday morning. He had cleared his diary for the weekend ready for the final push towards his presentation. Just a few tweaks, some polishing, some practising of the techie side and he'd be good to go. But it was such a fine sunny morning with a gentle breeze blowing in at the balcony that he decided the best way to start the day was with a swim at the gym. He threw a few things into his sports bag – cycling and running shorts, a fresh T-shirt, and a snack bar or two just in case he felt the need.

So at 9.45 when he'd already done his lengths and was feeling invigorated he decided to capitalise on the morning by dropping down to the gym basement and taking out on of the hire bikes for a quick ride. Not something he did as often as he should, but good for the old heart when he did manage to make time – and there was time enough this morning for a ride and then get back to work, wasn't there? And couldn't he run through his presentation mentally as he went? Physicality was good for creativity, after all.

On a day like today wouldn't it be nice to follow the river?

Upstream or downstream? He cycled down through Greenwich Park towards the Thames; one direction would take him to Deptford the other towards Woolwich. Deptford had once been the site of docks for the most powerful navy in the world – so important it even attracted young Tsar Peter the Great to come and work there, learning from the ground up how to create his own navy. He also got into trouble for trashing his lodgings and running wild wheelbarrow races in the gardens, as Declan recalled with amusement. But that was not what he was supposed to be thinking about this morning. He switched gears, speeded up, and headed along the river path, feeling a pleasant glow of muscle power being stretched. And began running through his presentation material…

*

After three quarters of an hour his muscles were beginning to complain just a little, and his mind even more. He'd been considering which of the early case studies were vital to his paper and which were peripheral. And how far back to go? By now the Beast of Gevaudan (1764) and its spate of gory killings had been in and out so many times it seemed to be dancing some kind of historical hokey cokey. But was it necessary for contextualising his lycanthropy theory?

Oh God, was that the time already? Better get some lunch. Declan turned around and began cycling back up to the gym.

*

Having returned the bike, picked up a baguette and roast chicken pie on the way home, Declan slumped on the sofa with a large mug of tea. His calves were aching and he felt justified in taking a break before he fired up the laptop and started work. At least he'd made a decision about the Beast of Gevaudan. Definitely out for good. Maybe after a brief nap…

Later, quite a bit later, he sat up, wondering what had woken him. It was the answerphone ringing. He did not get that many calls on the landline but he kept it on mainly for his mother and a couple of old aunties who tended to call on the weekend. Must have missed them. But when he checked, there was no message left other than a man's voice saying *Hello?* Well, if it was important he'd ring back. More likely a scammer telling him his internet was about to be disconnected or his Amazon account had been compromised. So, back to work, and then maybe a takeaway for dinner. And that was Saturday taken care of. Plenty of time tomorrow for that final push.

*

By Sunday evening Declan had to admit he was in trouble. Another day of swimming, cycling, supermarket shopping, catching up with the washing and tumble drying that always seemed to take forever, and walking round the table avoiding the laptop. He had to admit that he'd developed diversionary techniques into a fine art. Oh God! Only one thing to do now – call in professional assistance.. He picked up his phone and texted: Help!

*

'I wondered how long it would take you to call,' said Ted, standing in the doorway twenty minutes later.

'Don't be such a smug bastard!'

'We were supposed to run through this on Friday night after dinner. Why did you slope off so early? Was it something I said?' asked Ted, walking into the flat and taking a seat by the table with Declan's laptop. He flipped it open and turned it on with an enquiring glance at Declan.

'Nothing you said. Just that I didn't want to spoil a nice evening with work stuff. Thanks for coming over, sorry if I'm keeping you away from dinner?'

'No problem. Alison's putting the girls to bed early then she'll be watching some God-awful girly thing on Netflix with Cass. Christmas movies are the worst – do you know they start showing them now the day after Halloween? We've had a busy day – took the kids to that adventure play park with the big pool and a flume, then I treated the family to a roast at the pub. They do good size portions there, couldn't eat another thing today. OK, so let me skim through the text then we'll run through the techie stuff together. That's what's putting the shits up you, isn't it?'

'You know me so well.'

'That one time things went a bit up the creek with PowerPoint – it wasn't *so* bad.'

'It was horrendous, you know it was,' said Declan, bringing up the files onscreen for Ted. 'There, this is the intro – no, that bit's gone, let me delete it. OK. There you go.'

Ted scrolled through the material with a quick professional eye, then sat back and nodded. 'This hasn't changed much since last time I read it, has it? Just needs a bit of refining. And your visual stuff is fine. Let's you and me just run it through – stand over there and give me the spiel.'

Declan did as he was told and was just beginning to relax into his performance when Ted stopped him.

'Good enough is good enough. Just remember to breathe, take your pauses when you need them, and try to – well, try to make it a bit more entertaining?'

'Entertaining?'

'This is a dinner; people want to relax and enjoy – this is a taster of what you can offer. Your real work comes when you get the funding for some serious research – and I've told you how you can do that.'

'I'm still thinking about it,' said Declan.

'OK,' said Ted, 'I'll just run through PowerPoint with you, then we're done.'

*

Half an hour later they were sitting at the table with a beer and a Chinese takeaway. Just a few spareribs, some Chow Mien, Hot and Sour soup, Egg Fried Rice, and if you threw in spring rolls and a Bang-Bang chicken you got free delivery.

'Mmn, are you going to eat that last rib?' asked Ted.

'Have it. I owe you; I couldn't do this without you.'

'Don't be silly. You know your stuff inside out. God, *I* know it inside out too! I don't understand why you're so anxious.'

'Murphy's Law?'

'Bollocks,' said Ted and ate the last spare rib. But they both knew that the one immutable Law of the Universe is Murphy's Law: *Anything that can go wrong will go wrong.*

Chapter 15

Little Red

The nightmares were becoming worse, much worse. For the past couple of nights, she had been afraid to go to sleep. The book on mindfulness lay on the bedside table, along with Dion Fortune's *Psychic Self-Defense*, both equally useless. By Monday night, bone tired and weary, Cass found herself drifting into scenes of bloody horror that woke her with a gasp but no clear memory of what she'd witnessed. She only knew that her wolf had been at the heart of it, more solid and more violent than before.

She picked up her phone and started texting Declan, reaching out for a touch of support and comfort. She might have mentioned a nightmare, or a – what do you call it? Hallucination? But they could talk about that tomorrow – oh, it was tomorrow... she hadn't realised how late it was... or how early. Declan's text was brief and reassuring; they'd have time to work through this tomorrow. Meanwhile, a cup of tea? That was always his go-to remedy at four in the morning...

*

Tuesday was probably the worst day of the week to try to fit in her consultation with Declan, but Cass wasn't going to give it up for anyone, even though she'd have to be straight on a train into town for a meeting at Soho House at three. Neil had called her in for a meeting about the shampoo commercial, and she wasn't going to give that up either.

Dressed for business, with her best killer heel shoes, and with a good foundation covering the bags under her eyes, she presented herself at reception as early as possible, and was buzzed straight in, with a sideways look from Marge.

Declan was at his desk, with a sandwich and a bottle of water in front of him. It might be unprofessional but he was starving. 'Come on in and take a seat,' he said.

'Thanks for seeing me now,' said Cass, sitting down opposite.

'I thought we could use a bit of extra time, if you don't mind watching me eat lunch. Your text made it seem pretty urgent? This hypnogogic hallucination?'

'I'm sorry, I just needed to talk…'

'That's what we're here for – you don't have to apologise. Go ahead and tell me whatever you want to. I'm listening.'

And she talked. She told him the whole saga of conjuring up a wolf *tulpa*, that night at the unit hotel. And the more she talked the more ludicrous it sounded, even to her own ears.

'It's not a hallucination, it's real,' she tried to explain, 'I hadn't much idea what a real wolf looks like, I've never seen one in real life, so my dream-wolf looks like an Alsatian – or a Teveuren.'

'A what?'

'A great big Belgian Shepherd dog, like the one next door

that gets into the garden – that's what my dream wolf looks like.

'Go on.'

'You don't believe a word I'm saying, do you? '

'I believe it's real to *you* but couldn't it seem equally real to you if it were the product of a drunken dream – or maybe you did see an Alsatian dog running loose in the hotel grounds? The two things became conflated?'

Cass reached into her bag for *Psychic Self-Defense* and pushed it across the desktop towards him. 'This book explains it far better than I can: a *tulpa* is a living thought form, the Tibetans still believe in it – read the section I've marked here.'

'You can't take this stuff seriously?'

'I need you to believe me and help me get this thing under control before it… it sucks the life out of me. It's feeding off my energy just like the *tulpa* of the Zen monk that Alexandra David-Neel created, or the wolf *tulpa* in this book. I can see it, touch it, smell it.'

'Look, you dream of a wolf; it scares you. You don't know what it means. But I can tell you, the subconscious mind thinks in clichés – you were tired, exhausted, frustrated – the wolf became a symbol of the anger you were unable to express. Our dreams and nightmares are full of big bad wolves and ogres and witches.'

'This isn't a fairy story!'

'On the contrary, it's the archetypal stuff of fairy stories. You're not going crazy, Cass, believe me. Many people experience animalistic delusions at some point in their lives, you are not alone. Why didn't you tell me any of this before?'

'If you don't believe me, you should ask that poor man in the laundrette.'

'What man?'

'The day of the thunderstorm – the man in the laundrette that my 'imaginary' wolf attacked. They had to take him off to hospital. I'm not the only one who can see it. I'm telling you, it's real. I think it's real – so it *is* real, isn't that what you said?'

'Wait a minute…. this man in the laundrette, was he on the large side, rather heavy? Slow speaking? I think I know who you mean,' said Declan. 'One of my patients got himself shut in a laundrette the other day. He said a dog wandered in off the street and gave him asthma. Or maybe it was the thunder and lightning that frightened him into a panic attack. He was a bit confused about the whole affair. Are you saying that you were there?'

'Yes, I called out the Fire Brigade and an ambulance.'

'You did all the right things. Well done!' His tone was friendly and ever so slightly patronising. 'I hear what you're saying but I can't believe there was a wolf, Cass, outside of your imagination. Can you accept that?'

Cass was beginning to feel fidgety, she had the feeling that he wasn't listening to her – oh, he heard what she said (what a bloody annoying phrase that was) but he wasn't really *listening*. He was *analysing* what she said, ticking little boxes and coming up with a theory to fit. A box to put her in – wasn't that the way this world worked, after all? But what if it was the wrong box? Like all those unwed mothers back in the nineteenth century who'd been diagnosed as 'moral defectives' and put into lunatic asylums for life without remission? Her own great-grandmother might have been one of those poor unfortunates, according to family lore, if she hadn't hidden her own illegitimate baby away in an attic until a shotgun wedding could be arranged. She wondered which box Declan was ticking now, as he scribbled something on a notepad.

'Do you ever experience feelings of déjà vu?' he asked her.

'Yes, doesn't everyone? Is that significant?'

'How often?

'Not very often. Occasionally. Why?

'Hmm… Would you be prepared to take an MRI scan?' Declan looked up at her with an encouraging expression.

'To see if I'm bonkers? Another neurotic woman?'

'Don't label yourself! There is a condition known as temporal lobe epilepsy that can have some very strange effects. Your GP could make the referral, and we'll get some tests done quickly?' Declan's voice was calm and reasonable and persuasive, and Cass had to admit that his professional judgment of the wolf situation was totally plausible, sane and logical. He had stripped away her craziness and offered a simple explanation to banish her fears and make her laugh at her anxieties. Almost. Because if there was no wolf *tulpa*, then what was it beneath the desk, growing more solid by the moment, gently rubbing its fur against her leg like a cat? The more she tried to dismiss it from her mind, the more real it became. Her dream-wolf, her nightmare, her darling.

'Too late anyway,' Cass sighed, and got up to leave. As she

made for the door she turned back and saw Declan's expression change to one of astonishment. She could see the wolf below the desk had started chewing the toe of one of his shoes. It was a nice, soft leather loafer.

'Sweet Jesus, what is that thing?' he said.

'Well, it's not a bloody great big Belgian Shepherd dog, is it?' said Cass, as the wolf pulled the loafer off Decan's foot and began running around the office with it. Wolves, foxes and dogs are all playful creatures at heart, after all. Shoes are fair game for stealing, chewing, and even pooing in if you leave them out in the garden overnight.

'Bad Boy! Drop it!' said Cass sternly, but her wolf was having too much fun. It leapt onto an ancient leather armchair in the corner of the office, still holding the shoe in its jaws, and knocked a couple of cushions onto the floor. Then it turned its attention from the shoe, and with a quick motion ripped up a cushion, sending a flurry of dusty old kapok into the air. It was having fun.

Declan picked up a heavy stapler from the desk and threw it at the wolf, hitting it on the flank. The wolf stopped cavorting joyfully in the kapok storm and snarled at Declan, who froze where he stood. Then the wolf snatched up the loafer again, gave it a good shake, and leapt towards the closed door – then sailed *through* it, leaving the shoe behind to fall to the ground with a soft clunk.

'He's gone,' said Cass, feeling drained. It had taken everything she had to keep the wolf playful.

'Jesus Mary Mother of God!' said Declan, staring wide-eyed. 'Could you do that again on camera for me?'

'*What?*' she said. Was he asking for a repeat performance?

He pushed his laptop across the desk to her and brought up some files, running through a series of photos. 'I've been researching lycanthropy and psychosis for years – look: Wolfman, Cat Woman, Gerbil boy?' Then the heavily tattooed Tiger Man came up and Cass shuddered.

'That's completely disgusting! Why would anyone want to do that to themselves? Oh, wait a minute – now I see why you're so interested in my Little Red Riding Hood Complex! You must think I'm like *them*?'

'Yours is the most amazing full-blown psychosis I've ever encountered; I need you in my case studies.'

'You want me to become another one of your human guinea pigs? No thanks! My name's not Daisy Gamble.'

'Daisy who?'

'Google it! Oh, forget it – just pretend we never met.'

'But I can use this research to help people like you – oh my God, Cass, you can even project your hallucinations.'

'Yeah,' she said, picking up his shoe on her way out of the door, and throwing it at him. 'And don't forget, my hallucinations have great big teeth – and plenty of slobber. You might want to wash that loafer before you put it back on!' And she stalked out of the office with great dignity, leaving her *Psychic Self-Defense* on his desk. So much for therapy; if there any solution to her problem she was going to have to find it for herself.

*

After a dash into town on a stuffy train and tube, Cass turned up at the Soho House meeting only to find it had been cancelled. Fuming, she was about to phone Neil when a text pinged into her mobile from him asking her to drop round the corner to one of the small film screening studios instead.

'Ah, darling! Pain about the meeting with Ozzy and the *DayDawn* people, but something came up. Anyway, now you're here come and see the first cut of the promo,' said Neil, waving her into the auditorium where lights were low and a few people she recognised, plus a couple she didn't, were already seated. Neil's partner Brian, the producer, was in the middle of a phone call, made a wry face at Cass and went on talking, something about: *Look, I'll walk the cheque over to your office myself if needs be.*

'Writers,' said Neil, 'always moaning about their bloody money! Nobody's been paid yet. Anyway, take a seat, Cass. I think you're going to like this. I think we'll take it to Berlin first – see what the Germans think? Bloody cold in February,' he added, as the music came up for promo.

Cass had to admit it wasn't totally crappy for a low budget slasher/horror of that ilk, but that really wasn't saying all that much. The scenes shot in 'Tibet' now featured a spookily shadowy CGI Zen Monk *tulpa*, who morphed into a real-life man when it followed Alexandra back to London. Now played by an actor with compelling ice blue eyes, the Monk became a kind of Jack the Ripper killing a variety of young women in an increasingly bizarre series of ritualistic murders. In desperation Alexandra was forced to return to Tibet –

interiors, not Welsh mountainsides this time – and use the age-old wisdom of the Shaman to conjure her *tulpa* out of existence. In a ritual of drumming and tasteful nudity, the murderous Monk became a wispy CGI figure once more and was reabsorbed into Alexandra's supine body along a silvery umbilical cord. All of this was presented in short scenes lifted from the film, whilst still in post-production.

'Not bad, eh?' said Neil, as the lights went up. 'Considering we've had to throw it together in a bit of a hurry?'

Cass agreed, and wondered to herself whether any of them would be getting paid any time soon? Not the writer, of course, he'd be bottom of the pile.

'Now, we start the *DayDawn* account next week,' said Neil. 'There'll be some real money in that, I promise you. I'm getting back all the old team – you, Animal, that good sound bloke, what'shisname – clear your diary from Monday onwards, I'll let you know as soon as the meeting with Ozzy's back on.'

'He is?'

'The big boss. Mr Shampoo himself.'

'Right,' said Cass and got up to leave. It hadn't been a totally wasted afternoon. She'd watched probably one of the worst promos she'd ever seen, with a ghastly soundtrack by what'shisname, but at least her wolf had not come out to play again. Maybe her mind needed distraction to keep the wolf at bay? She was too tired to think about it now, as she stood and swayed on the rush hour train in murderously spiky heels that were killing her. She'd think about it tomorrow, as Scarlet O'Hara had once said in a much better movie.

Chapter 16

Teddy Bears' Picnic

By Friday it was another bright, sunny morning in Greenwich Park as Alison and the other Toddler mums cleared up after their Teddy Bears' Picnic. Every small child's favourite Teddy had been hidden amongst the trees and bushes to be found by its devoted owner, there had been games, homemade cupcakes, no-added-sugar squash, and hardly any fractious tears from the small people. Now, herded back into people carriers, or buggies for the walkers, they were heading for home.

'Do you want a lift back?' asked Trudy, one of the playgroup leaders, as Alison helped her load equipment into the back of her vehicle. 'Come in for a quick coffee?'

'That would be nice, but I don't really have time to stop this morning. Could you take us up to the top of the Heath? We'll walk from there, it's nice weather.'

'I only hope it holds for another couple of weeks,' said Trudy, 'we're off to Devon on holiday. We're getting a dog when we come back. My boys have been pestering me for a puppy for ages, and now they've both started school, I think the time's right. The house seems so empty when I go home now, it would be company for me too.'

'Oh, that's nice, what sort of dog?' asked Alison, putting Debbie into one of the child car seats lined up in the back.

'A Labrador, or maybe a Golden Retriever. Not sure yet.'

'That's quite a big dog, isn't it? Hard to handle?'

'Oh, I can take it to dog training,' Trudy smiled. 'And I want a proper dog – not a toy – something that makes you feel safe, you know? There've been a couple of break-ins down our way: jewellery thieves would you believe?'

'Yes, I know what you mean; sometimes I wish Ted wasn't always working late or off to some conference or other whenever things happen – like one of the twins falling out of a tree, or Debbie swallowing a five pence coin! I had to drive her up to Casualty in the middle of the night and get Ted's mother over to babysit the girls. She was not best pleased about that.'

*

Alison waved goodbye to Trudy and unfolded the buggy at the edge of the Heath. She popped Debbie into it, already half asleep, and began to wheel it swiftly along the path that leads to the village. Skies were blue, the sun was warm, there was little traffic about. The odd car and a dirty white van stopped at the traffic lights behind them, the odd cyclist, and a Lycra clad runner passed her by. It was a pleasant walk and she really should do this more often, try to leave the car at home, think of the environment.

Cass was waiting in the doorway as Alison pushed the buggy in, with Debbie now spark out, drooling ever so slightly, with Little Ted wrapped in her arms.

'Back already?' said Alison. 'How's the flat?'

'Well,' said Cass, lifting Debbie out of the buggy gently without waking her, 'I went down this morning fearing the worst – and guess what? It's fine! I can move back in tomorrow. Then I stopped off for some retail therapy. Wait till you see what I found in that vintage shop.'

Alison put Debbie on her bed to finish her nap and came down to have a coffee with her sister just as Cass was pulling a pair of shoes out of a box and –

'Don't put them on the table! It's bad luck,' Alison shouted.

'That's only for *new* shoes; these are pre-loved, though I don't think they've ever been worn. Aren't they beautiful?'

Alison looked at the spiky heels and the trademark red soles and had to admit they were both beautiful *and* a bargain. 'But I thought you said you'd never wear heels again, it wasn't worth the agony?'

'Oh, that was yesterday. I'll take these along in my bag and wear trainers tomorrow. Going into Soho House again – the meeting's back on. Honestly, I might as well be a yo-yo. I hope it cools down a bit, the Tube's unbearable. I was bosom to bosom with that Mark Kermode on the Central Line the other day. It was so hot and sticky it's a wonder we weren't glued together for life. I couldn't keep my eyes off his hair – it never moves even when the Tube's lurching along.'

'I'm glad the flat's finally done,' said Alison, 'though I'm going to miss you.'

'I'm not going far, well not till the next job – God, I hope we're not away filming in the Brecon Beacons again. I'll find out tomorrow.'

*

Tomorrow was a cooler day and Cass shot off early, declining a lift from Ted, she declared that she could easily walk to the station in her trainers. She intended to keep fit. Alison wondered how long these good intentions would last but made no comment. She made the school run with Debbie in her booster seat along with the twins, dropped the girls off then went back home for a second breakfast. No Toddler Group today, so she had a free morning.

Alison was still eating a naughty croissant dipped in milky coffee when the land line rang and she ran to answer it before the wretched answerphone message kicked in. It was one of the other mums. Funny how when you had children you forfeited your own name and became Debbie's Mum, or Coraline's Mum, or Ben's Mum.

'I wanted to let you know before you heard it elsewhere,' said the voice on the phone, 'before it's on the News – something's happened along the Vale – something awful – are you still there?'

Alison had paused to draw a slow breath, she didn't want to ask but she had to: 'Yes, but someone should tell Trudy, that's where she lives, isn't it? Along the Vale?'

'It's Trudy that it happened to, Alison: she's dead. Someone broke into her home yesterday – they found out when she didn't collect the children from school.'

Alison sat down suddenly, and all the colour drained out of the day. Somehow the phone conversation ended with promises to be careful, and not to say anything to the children yet. What about Trudy's children, Alison thought, who was telling them what had happened to their mum?

She knew how this would play out today – they'd be besieged by the media, looking for a story, another Deptford Wolf slaying was always news, Neighbourhood Watch would descend on her for an Extraordinary Meeting as she was Acting Chair, so better get organised with tea and biscuits, cups and saucers…

She switched on the TV news channel in case there was anything relevant, but kept the sound turned off. Debbie was engrossed in a biscuit that she was feeding to a doll but would have to be kept occupied when the Neighbourhood Watch mob showed up. All this was running through Alison's mind as she emptied the dishwasher, as it struck her that she must have been the last person to see Trudy alive. What was it she'd been saying about getting a dog when they came back from their holiday? And Alison remembered smiling at the mental picture of petite, blonde Trudy in charge of a big black Labrador or some such large breed. Why on earth had they waited? Why not get a dog *now*? But now was already too late. Too late and too sad to think about, so she got on with unloading the dishwasher, phoning round the Neighbourhood Watch, and settling Debbie down to do some colouring in front of the TV in the girls' bedroom with the monitor screen on to keep an eye on her, when the Neighbourhood Watch ladies arrived.

*

By late afternoon when Cass got back, it was all over the news: *the Deptford Wolf strikes again.* She let herself in quietly, went into the kitchen where Alison was tidying up after feeding the children, and gave her a hug. Alison burst into tears.

'It's OK, it's Kk,' said Cass. 'You're allowed to be sad –'

'No. it's *not* OK– and I'm not sad, I'm *angry!* It's so unfair – Trudy never gets to see her kids grow up, never sees their graduation day, their wedding day. All those wonderful, special days: he stole all that from her.' Alison's whole body was shaking with furious sobs. Tears were bursting out of her, out of her eyes, down her nose, running down her cheeks.

'If I'd gone back with her for coffee, maybe –'

'Don't be crazy! You and Debbie? No! Better you didn't go.' Cass tried to hold her sister in her arms, but Alison pushed her away. This kind of anger was something Cass hadn't seen for a while, not since they were kids. It would subside in a while, she knew, Alison would let it out in one violent burst, then it would be over. She didn't hoard her anger, storing it up like Cass did, until it festered into something venomous.

Eventually the sobbing calmed down a little, and Alison grabbed some kitchen roll to clean her face up.

'The News said it was another Deptford Wolf murder, but it can't be, can it? It's not full moon, is it?' said Cass.

'They should consult Mrs McBride – *she* got it from Mrs O'Hanlon, and *she* got it from the old lady who lives next door, who got it from the Community Police Officers who came round – it was an opportunistic break-in while everyone was out; there have been a few of them in the area recently.

When Trudy came back early she must have surprised him. He probably didn't even mean to kill anyone – just panicked and that was that.'

'So what happens now?'

'We all stay vigilant – that's what they told us at our emergency meeting today. And those who can afford burglar alarms and camera doorbells are advised to install them. I hope you've got an alarm at yours?'

'Something along those lines,' said Cass, trying to reassure her. 'And new mortice locks that Mr Barycz fixed up for me.'

'I wish you'd stay here, Cass. Just a little bit longer?'

'No, I appreciate the offer – but I want to get my place sorted out now that the builders have left. You'll be all right, won't you? I'll stay till Ted gets home.'

'You'll stay and have dinner,' said Alison firmly, 'there's apple pie and custard for dessert.' And there was no arguing with that.

*

It was later than she thought when Ted dropped her home in the Porsche and Cass finally turned the key in her own front door to go back into her flat. It was clean, it was empty, everything looked perfect, if a trifle sparsely furnished. Never mind, Japanese minimalism was to be her new style after the divorce. She went into the bedroom, rolled out her duvet that had been thoroughly dried and nicely bagged up for her, and bounced on the mattress.

Lying on the bed, staring up at the ceiling, Cass felt a pang of sorrow for Alison, and for that dead woman she had never known. Alison's fury seemed so much more powerful and legitimate than her own anger in response to the string of petty frustrations that had birthed her dream-wolf. Her irritation was less than a pale shadow of Alison's rage and surely more easily manageable? She closed her eyes and visualised the wolf, clear in every detail. The long, lean body, the harsh fur, the head that looked something like a Husky and something like that Teveuren thing from next door – it didn't matter if it was an inexact approximation of a wolf, did it? It was *her* wolf.

And then there it was, there was her *tulpa* wolf, lying beside her bed, as she had first imagined it, but tied to her own body with some kind of silvery psychic cord; how strange that she'd never noticed it before. So all she had to do was exercise her will to draw it back into herself, wasn't it? Hadn't Declan said it was no more than a cliché? A symbol of repressed anger? Well then, let's accept that anger, let's *welcome* it in, let's stop thinking in clichés and fairy tale monsters.

Cass picked up a pillow and threw it across the room, but the wolf merely shook itself and settled down again, with its muzzle on its paws. She chucked another pillow as violently as she could. Not enough. Not nearly enough. Her anger might not be as pure and noble as Alison's but surely it could be just as fiery? Think of all the irritations of life mounting up over the years, getting under your skin, itching to be expressed? From the minor niggles such as Bombay Sapphire gin turning out *not* to be blue as it poured into the tall glass, to the more recent annoyance of being passed over for yet another job you knew you were perfect for, to the anguish of a break-up that you always knew was on the cards but still hurt like hell when it came? Jesus, wasn't all that enough to try the patience of a fucking saint? As she dug deeper into herself, Cass began to feel the heat of real honest to goodness anger rising, like poisonous crystals sublimating into toxic fumes.

Now the wolf pricked up its ears, leapt from the floor and shook out its body, performing the little dance of joy you often see from canines who know they are about to be fed. And she was ready to feed him all her anger, as rage flooded through her limbs until she felt she could tear the place apart with her bare hands. This was more like it! She wanted to smash windows for the sound of breaking glass, rip up the duvet and send feathers flying into the air, and scream till the neighbours called out the police – fortunately there were no neighbours since the old lady upstairs had passed, and something of her old self prevented any damage coming to the precious duvet. Instead, Cass went into the kitchen, picked up the nearest pots and pans and threw them at the wall. Still not enough. She opened a cupboard full of mismatched crockery – oh yes! She began lobbing cups at the wall, and the anger inside her began boil over with every delicious smash of cheap china against plasterboard. Angry? She could be angry: she could be furious, and maybe it was all right to be angry? And she realised that the wolf was not something she needed any more. Slowly the silvery umbilical that joined the two of them began to pulse and draw substance away from the *tulpa* with every shattered cup and plate.

Eventually when there was little left to smash, she looked around, only to see the barest shadow of a lupine shape in the doorway that flickered and faded into nothing. 'I better clean this lot up,' she said to the faint ghost of a wolf.

Feeling exhausted, and back on her bed again, Cass was tempted to phone Alison and tell her the *tulpa* problem was solved. But now was not the time. She remembered when she first told Alison about the *tulpa*, how Alison had laughed and said if you really could conjure up anything, why on earth not make some more appealing imaginary friends? A Brad Pitt look-alike? Or a Daniel Craig? Or anyone else you might fancy, come to that?

Cass smiled and wondered what it would be like to have your own private Brad Pitt at your beck and call? Or maybe someone like Declan O' Neil? What would he feel like, she wondered, if she conjured him up? He'd be gentle, warm; a misty shape that took flesh and became real ... A nice suit, a better haircut, shave a couple of years off him, and airbrush few of the careworn lines from around the eyes and wouldn't he be the perfect man? She imagined nestling up to him on her bed, and him rubbing her back – he had nice hands, he'd be good at massaging all the tension out of her spine – and it was a long time since anyone had done that. She yawned and began drifting into that comfortable state between dozing and dreaming. She could almost feel the warmth of his body next to hers... She almost reached out to him...Then the doorbell rang. And rang again.

Cass opened her eyes and was relieved to see that there

was no one else in the room. No imaginary friends or fiends this time. She went to answer the door, wondering who on earth was calling at this time of night. Outside it was raining heavily, and there was a man, wearing a rather shabby, badly fitting old raincoat, holding something wrapped in a plastic carrier bag under his arm. It was Declan O'Neil, looking very wet. 'Can I come in?' he said.

Chapter 17

Carnival Street

The couple of days since that session with Cass had passed in a kind of fog, as Declan struggled to get his head around what exactly had happened. He went over his own research material again and again, but there was nothing remotely helpful. He searched online for anything on *tulpa* – thought the first thing that came up was some publicity material for what looked like a cheap horror film. Of course, it was that production she'd been working on, the thing that had started all this – this madness. Not a word he used lightly, but in this case perhaps it was justifiable. There were a few more serious articles, some historical material, but nothing scientific, nothing giving a rational explanation for what he'd actually seen – and felt when he'd put his soggy shoe back on.

Declan was a great believer in rational explanations, always had been, even when he was a teenager hooked on one of those insidious part-works that entrapped you with continuing features on unexplained mysteries such as The Cottingly Fairies, the Case of the Croglin Vampire, or Lucy Lightfoot, who had apparently vanished into a time-slip vortex in a small church on the Isle of Wight. The weekly magazines offered intriguing pseudo-scientific explanations for such phenomena. But now when you Googled them you were more likely to find that these fantastical tales were exactly that – fictions dreamed up by a local curate, or a piece of trick photography from a couple of imaginative schoolgirls. He even found himself looking up that name Cass had thrown at him: *Daisy Gamble* – and that search turned out to be rather more informative than anticipated.

But eventually he had to put his thoughts aside and focus on the daily mix of work (with interruptions from on high) routine paperwork, reports, and meetings that seemed repetitions of last month's or last year's meetings eating into his time. Back at home he usually found himself dozing off at the kitchen table over his laptop, once over his dinner. Most of the Chinese take-away ended up in his lap that evening.

By Friday night Declan was beginning to feel he'd never be ready for the presentation dinner at the end of the month, so what did it matter if he'd still not picked up that black tie suit from the hire place? The ticket was still in his trouser pocket, he could feel the sharp edge of it reproaching him as he shifted his weight. His neck was aching from poring over his notes, maybe he could grab a few moments' rest on the old sofa.

Stretching out along the squishy-squashy cushions that were a legacy from a past girlfriend, he began relaxing for a moment. His mind drifted back once again to Cass and her wolf. Something had happened, he was sure of that, but quite what was less clear to him now. A shared delusion? *Folie a deux?* If it was an example of the personal fable, the belief that there is something special and unique about yourself, then Cass had it in spades. But don't we all think we are the lead role in our own lives? Hamlet, not Rosencrantz and Guildenstern? Though to be fair, Rosencrantz and Guildenstern did graduate to starring in a play of their own, though that drama ended no better than Hamlet's. *The rest is silence…* or something like that.

Declan turned over, getting comfortable, and found that somehow, he'd managed to undress himself and slip between the cool sheets of his own bed. This was so much better than dozing on the lumpy old sofa. Somehow it did not surprise him that Cass, equally naked, was lying in bed beside him. It seemed so natural, the scent of her hair, the feel of her skin beneath his hands. He felt the touch of her lips on his and closed his eyes as she straddled him, leaning on his shoulders with her hands pinning him to the bed. Somehow this all felt very natural too, as the bodies blended in a dreamlike passion, and he felt her warm tongue licking his cheek. This seemed like something that had happened before, rather than for the first time, as the old song goes – what *was* that song? As her body rippled over his, Declan opened his eyes and looked up into the eyes of the woman he loved.

Her eyes were the yellow eyes of a wolf, and the grey pelt of a wolf spread down over her shoulders as her visage transformed into the head of a wolf. *What big teeth you have, Grandmother… All the better to eat you with…* As the wolf-woman jaws lunged towards him, Declan woke up with a half scream in his throat and rolled off the sofa along with the squishy-squashy cushions onto the floor. God, that was a real Jungian one for the books! Those cushions had to go, along with other mementos of girlfriends past that were taking up space, like the electric knife sharpener sitting on the worktop unopened. He wiped the image of the wolf-woman from his mind and went to make himself a cup of tea.

As he took a comforting sip of green tea, he absent-mindedly picked up the copy of Dion Fortune's *Psychic Self-Defense* lying on the table where he'd left it earlier. There was something about a wolf *tulpa* in here that Cass told him to read. He'd bought the book ages ago as a curiosity, flipped through it but never read it properly. He opened it and left it on the counter as he drank another sip of tea. Left to their own devices the leaves of the book fluttered and settled of their own accord at the fly leaf – with the name *Cassandra Green* scrawled in black biro across it, with an address in Carnival Street, Greenwich. Declan went over to the desk and opened the top drawer – there lay his own copy of *Psychic Self-Defense*, where it had always been. Somehow he'd acquired her book too. And the thought struck him that maybe he should return it? And that there was no time like the present, was there? Since she had not answered any of his calls or texts, he might as well take the risk. It was only a quarter past eight. It was only drizzling a bit. He put on a mac and shoved the book into a plastic bag that had previously held a take-away-for-one but didn't smell of curry anymore.

*

'Can I come in?' he said, as Cass opened the front door to him.

The rain was now beating down in stair rods and he was very wet. Parking the bus in Carnival Street was out of the question, permit holders only, and he'd had to walk from the car park at the other end of beyond. What had seemed like a good idea at the time, did not seem like such a good idea at all now.

She stared at him for a moment, said: 'OK.' and led him into the flat. 'I suppose you want your money. I still owe you for two sessions.'

'You left your book at the hospital.' He held out a plastic carrier bag with her copy of *Psychic Self-Defense*. 'I thought I should return it.'

'At this time of night?' Cass looked sceptical. 'Thanks. You better take your mac off, let's put it by the gas fire – I'll turn it on for a minute.' She took his mac and spread it over the back of a chair in front of the gas fire to dry. 'So what's this really about? You doctor chaps don't go making house calls for nothing?'

'Look, something happened to us – something I can't explain yet.'

'Don't worry about it; I've dealt with it. Got rid of it. Turns out my wolf wasn't as big and bad after all.'

'You still believe it's something outside yourself?'

'Not anymore. I imagined it into existence, so I imagined it *out* of existence. I have a bin full of broken crockery to prove it.'

'What?'

'Never mind.' She preferred not to go into details about how she'd nicked the idea of reabsorbing her wolf from a movie, working title: *Tulpa Terror*. 'It's gone for good, believe me.'

'I wish I could be so sure. I'm concerned about you, Cass.'

'I'm not your problem anymore – and I'm certainly not your guinea pig,' she added.

'Maybe I was wrong about putting you in my research project,' Declan admitted. 'I'm sorry if it upset you. I…um… I Googled *Daisy Gamble*. Turns out she's a character in a Barbra Streisand musical?'

'*On a Clear Day You Can See Forever*. With Yves Montand as the psychiatrist she engages to cure her of chain smoking. Only that's not all he does, is it? He hypnotises her back into a past life when her name was 'Melinda Tentrees'. Lovely sets and costumes, weren't they?'

'He'd be struck off for conducting that kind of regression therapy without her knowledge or permission.'

Cass burst out laughing. 'It was a musical, not a documentary!'

'Even so, it was a breach of patient / therapist relationship – *she* starts falling in love with him, and *he* starts fancying her previous incarnation as some glamorous Regency lady swanning around Brighton Pavilion. You'd be struck off for that too.'

'But did you like the film? It was one of Armistead Maupin's favourites.'

'I only read the synopsis and watched some clips – I didn't have time to take in the whole thing.'

'Pity. Not one of Barbra's very best, but I liked it; part of my childhood education. When I was a toddler my Mum's idea of childcare was to sit me in a playpen in front of the TV to watch whatever daytime movies were on – old black and white comedies, romances, MGM musicals. I think that's what made me want to go into the film business. I wanted to make wonderful musicals too. But I end up making crappy horror films and ads for haemorrhoids and hairspray.'

'Cass, I'm sorry if you thought I was trying to exploit you in any way. But can't you see how amazing this thing is? This thing you can do with your mind? Christ, you could make a film of that, couldn't you!'

'So this time you thought you'd hit the jackpot? Psychiatry doesn't pay as well as neurosurgery, I suppose.'

'What's that go to do with it?'

'Ah, don't tell me you didn't want to be a brain surgeon, but you couldn't get the grades? Like your best mate Ted? Allie told me all about it years ago.'

'I've never wanted to be a brain surgeon – or a rocket scientist, or even be in a boy band! I just wanted to help people,' he said. And that was the truth, even though he often doubted the capacity of the mental health services to always offer adequate help. Even so, he could only do what he could do and hope it would be enough.

'I still owe you for two consultations,' said Cass, going to her bag and pulling out a new fifty pound note with the image of Alan Turing. She pushed it towards him; but Declan waved it away.

'It's on the house.'

'Take it!' she said. So he took it, pushing it into his trouser pocket where he could feel a reproachful dig from the Moss Bros card.

'Now we're quits,' said Cass. 'I'm no longer your patient. *This* is from the little Goth Girl…' and she reached up on tiptoes to take his face in her hands and kiss him on the mouth. Her breath smelt of apples and cloves, sweet and astringent at the same time. 'And *this* is from me,' she said and boxed him on the ears. Declan recoiled in surprise at the sharp sting of pain. 'What was that for?' he asked.

'To remind you to listen to your clients – not just analyse them – *listen* to what they are actually saying, and you might learn something. And the next time someone tells you they have created a *tulpa*, you better believe them, because it won't be me; it might be some psycho with an agenda.'

'I'll try to remember that,' said Declan ruefully, rubbing the side of his head. She was small, but she was hard-hitting in more ways than one. He took his mac, still gently steaming, from the chair by the gas fire and headed for the door. Cass opened it for him. It had double locks and a chain, he noted, though she didn't seem to use the chain.

'Cass, please, if you ever need any help…?'

'I know, I call you or send a text. Goodbye Dr O'Neil.'

'Oh, by the way,' he added, pausing halfway out of the door. 'I preferred the little Goth Girl.' And he went into the street with a faint taste of apple and cloves on his lips. At least the rain had stopped, he thought to himself, as he turned down his damp collar and walked back to the car park. She was right about one thing, he thought, she was no longer his patient. But she was something. Something he wouldn't forget in a hurry.

Chapter 18

Mr Shampoo

Brookwood Cemetery is the largest cemetery in Western Europe, once the largest in the world. The adjoining military sections are neat and well kept, whilst the older Victorian cemetery itself is a gothic wilderness of vines, ivy and broken graves. Or so it was when Cass and the crew began setting up the *DayDawn* shoot on a grey morning. They had hacked their way through to the chosen spot trailing cable to set up lights and cursing the stinging nettles that somehow penetrated even the toughest trouser legs. Animal was one of the few who seemed impervious to the stings and arrows – or was it slings and arrows? – as he made his way through the undergrowth. Why the hell Neil had hired him again was beyond Cass, but that was his choice.

'Why don't I ever see you around?' Animal had asked as soon as he'd arrived on location in his grimy old white van. 'I'm only down the road from you in Woolwich.'

'I haven't been staying at my flat, I had the builders in,' she'd replied.

'What d'you want to go an' get builders in for? Me and some of the lads could do any little jobs for you,' he'd said and handed her a card that declared *no job too small or too big.*

140

Cass had thanked him and put the card in a pocket to be disposed of later. With any luck she'd never find herself on another crew with Animal after today.

*

It was three weeks since the night when she had conquered her demons and Declan O'Neil had turned up on her doorstep uninvited, wet and bedraggled. Since then most of the past events had vanished from her mind like a dream at dawn. Dreams cannot be trusted. For instance, every now and then when she was tired, between sleeping and waking, a brief image might come to her – perhaps a flash of a row of brick buildings glimpsed from a train in Berlin one sunny day – Cass knew she'd taken a sightseeing trip with friends the last time she'd been working over there, but was this a true memory or merely a scene from a film –*The Bourne Identity?* As a child she'd been given a book on the wonders of the ancient world, stories of the most amazing places and the men who'd discovered them, or lied about discovering them, and in her mind's eye she had visited Palmyra – Tadmor in the Wilderness – and stood in the footsteps of Queen Zenobia, and seen the rose pink rock-hewn city of Petra in visions so real that she wondered if she'd been there in some earlier life? Cass had to admit to herself that perhaps Declan had been right to be sceptical about her wolf *tulpa,* maybe it was a temporary madness they'd shared for a moment? That's how she was beginning to see things now – and beginning to regret sending Declan off with a flea in his ear. Anyway, the wolf was gone, gone for good, life was back to normal, and she was back in the world of work. Reasonably well-paid work for a change.

*

Jimbo, with a gentleman's black frock coat slung over one skinny arm, strolled over to Cass. He heaved a sigh and shook his head. 'It's déjà vu all over again, innit?' he said, 'Same old merry team, another nasty, spooky location.'

'Where's Mac then?' asked Cass.

'Benidorm, gone to visit her sister. She'll be enjoying the sunshine.'

'At least we've got a Portaloo. And look – the sun's coming out, it'll be a nice day. And think of the dosh.'

'I *do*, I do – but I'd still rather not be stuck in the middle of Surrey Puma country.'

'What? Oh, come on, Jimbo, not another one of your ridiculous urban myths!'

'It's not urban and it's not a myth,' he said huffily, 'It's on YouTube and everything. At least 400 sightings of a mystery big cat around Brookwood and places like Croydon.'

'Croydon? Now you *are* pulling my leg.'

'Well, maybe it was the Phantom Cat Killer in Croydon,' he said. 'Oops, I better go and look after my artiste. He can get a bit antsy if he's left for too long.' And Jimbo wandered off again with a weary little wave of the hand.

Cass checked her watch and glanced at the three *DayDawn* Girls who were sitting in a row of canvas chairs bearing the familiar double D logo that always put her in mind of heavily underwired bras for the well-endowed rather than expensive hair product. Buzzing around them was the little Makeup Girl and their personal Stylist, a thin, harassed looking young woman with a couple of bulky holdalls at her feet. The DD Girls were a blonde, a brunette and a redhead, each with impossibly long glossy hair, a tribute to *DayDawn* products. Tall, slim, and well-groomed, there they sat waiting like greyhounds at the slips, or whatever it was. So long as they continued waiting patiently and didn't get antsy like Jimbo's male artiste that was all OK.

'Cass, where's the Gaffer gone now? He was here a minute ago,' the Director padded over in a panic. 'It's going to be a disaster.'

'No, he's only in the Portaloo, he'll be back in a tic. But I did warn you about hiring caterers on the cheap. Don't stress, everything's under control.'

'You don't understand, I've had a call from Ozzie – he's coming down to take a look – says he was in the vicinity – I don't believe a word – he's checking up on us – fuck, I hate it when clients do that.'

'Neil, breathe – slowly – that's it, now take it easy, we'll be set up and good to go on schedule.'

'But Ozzie will be here any minute now!'

'Then we'll deal with him when he gets here.' Cass had met Ozzie briefly at the re-scheduled client meeting. *DayDawn* was his latest business acquisition and he wanted to relaunch the range with a fresh, quirky kind of image. He was younger than she'd anticipated, and well-spoken as you might expect of public school educated minor Arab royalty. Which royal family was it he sprang from? Somewhere in the Emirates? She had no idea, but he'd struck her as rather like the young Omar Sharif emerging from a glimmering desert mirage in

Lawrence of Arabia.

'Oh, my God, he's here!' gasped Neil, clutching her arm. Cass turned to see a couple of figures walking up to the clearing in front of the gravestone and family tomb chosen as their site – Ozzie and a dark suited man who walked ahead of him, swishing the stinging nettles away with a rolled umbrella.

'Good morning, Neil!' Ozzie called out to them, waving and smiling. So far so good.

'Ozzie! You've found us!' Neil scrambled down the path to greet him and Cass followed.

'You remember my right-hand girl, Cass?' said Neil, shaking hands with Ozzie, as the dark suited man with the umbrella dropped back at a gesture from his master. Must be the chauffeur, thought Cass. Or a bodyguard.

'Lovely to meet you again. How's it going?' asked Ozzie, casting a glance around, and noting the three *DayDawn* Girls sitting on their canvas chairs. 'Ah, I see you have the redhead too. The three of them make a lovely picture, don't they? We'll be selecting a new set of models for our Afro product range soon – we'll be looking for a different campaign image there.'

'Yeah, well, we'll be very happy to move on with that as soon as you want,' said Neil. 'Would you, um, like to stay for a while?'

'Oh, just a few moments – perhaps see a little bit of the magic you do?'

'Cass, get some chairs – over there – we can run through a quick rehearsal of the first couple of shots,' Neil hissed. Cass called to Animal to rustle up some chairs and a drink for their guest. Animal was quick to set up a couple more canvas seats and hurried back to fetch a flask of coffee from the caterers. He positioned himself behind Ozzie, as if waiting for further missions to be accomplished. Cass shot him a glance, but he was either too thick to take a hint and get lost, or he intended to stay and earwig.

Ozzie sat through a brief couple of shots, taking a few pictures on his phone of 'his girls'. He seemed to be enjoying himself as he watched the Vampire – Jimbo's artiste – step out of the shadow of the family vault, loom over the flat tombstone where not one but *three* Maidens were lying helplessly waiting for his ungodly attentions. But as bright sunlight – provided by the Sparks – illuminated the scene, each Maiden rose from the tomb, swung out her glossy tresses so that sunlight could stream though her hair, turning the Vampire into crumbling dust. And that's the power of *DayDawn* shampoo, thought Cass. True the Vampire was in a fit of the sulks, and the girls were a bit wooden after sitting around in the cold, but they'd done their best, and she hoped that would be good enough, or Neil might have a coronary. And she didn't want to have to pick up the pieces.

'I love it,' Ozzie smiled. 'That's it! That's why I hired you boys, for something quirky, a little bit camp – do we still say *camp*? Something a bit rough around the edges like a student film. No one wants to hear their shampoo is full of 'botanicals', or marshmallow cream, or all that laurel sodium stuff. I want *DayDawn* to be about *fun*.'

'Absolutely,' Neil agreed. Ozzie took a couple of small gold edged cards out of his pocket and handed them to Neil and Cass.

'I'm having a little party next week, a few people in the beauty business. Love to have you there, Neil, and you Cass? Please feel free to bring along a plus one.' And with that Ozzie smiled at her, turned and waved at 'his girls' and took his leave, with Umbrella Man leading the way down the path.

'Oh, my God, Oh, my God, Oh, my God,' said Neil. 'He liked it – it was a mess, but he liked it.' He sat down heavily on a chair. 'You've got to come to that party, Cass, he likes you – he's got a thing for redheads. Charm him, you're good at that – what? You don't have to screw him, or anything – oh, no, I mean, not unless you *wanted* to – oh, God, I can't cope with gender politics anymore.'

'Don't have to say anything, Neil, I know what you mean, you'd like some moral support – and you'd like the contract for the Afro products commercial.'

'Yes!' said Neil.

'But it's in the middle of Canary Wharf, and I haven't got my new car yet.'

'I can take you, Flash,' Animal stepped in quickly. 'I'll be your plus-one.'

'What?'

'Yes,' said Neil. 'Cass, please, I need you there, Brian and I *rely* on you – you know we do.'

'I'll drive you, sweetheart, no problem,' said Animal. 'Look, I'll even get the van cleaned before the weekend.'

'Have you even got anything to wear to a party like this?' said Cass. More or less a rhetorical question. Neil pulled quite a few notes out of his wallet and pushed them into her hands.

'Get him a suit, or whatever he needs, and get him a

haircut,' he said, with a look at Animal. 'And for heaven's sake get yourself a car on the road as soon as you can.'

Cass took the notes and stuffed them into a pocket. Perhaps after all Ozzie's party would distract her mind from those last, lingering thoughts of Declan O'Neil and a kiss that she probably should have left un-kissed. And Ozzie was rather gorgeous, even if he was just another client with more money than taste. But for now, it was back to work. It was *DayDawn,* and *DayDawn* was fun!

Chapter 19

Gentrification

Cass was staring out of the tiny kitchen sink window of her flat. A small, paved area and a scrubby patch of grass was all that remained of what once must have been a garden. She was washing up the rather nice Royal Worcester Jamie Oliver Snug Cup and saucer that she used for her morning coffee, having picked up a set of two from a charity shop. An unopened, unwanted gift, she presumed, as they were still in their original packaging. The sort of thing you might give to a couple for an engagement present, or a low budget wedding gift. A broken engagement? A cancelled wedding? Why did that run through her mind? She dismissed the thought. She'd made several trips to local charity shops over the past weeks to replace all the crockery she'd smashed. Blackheath had some particularly classy shops, and there was Greenwich market for vintage stuff. She'd been away from home long enough to be struck by the way gentrification had pulled up the old places remembered from childhood.

Mind you, Blackheath had always been posh compared to Lewisham where the Pratts lived. Back in the day she and Alison had walked up the long roads to go up to the Heath or took the bus to Greenwich Park for a treat. What was the name of that road they always used to laugh at? Snat Hatcher? Why was it called that? Oh, yes, it was 'Hat Snatcher Road' – where once, after the Second World War, their grandmother had been mugged by a man who snatched her new hat and made off with it. She was so shocked and befuddled when she told her family of the attack that it came out as *Snat Hatcher*.

Cass was not much given to reminiscing, but this morning had started off badly with sorting out a box of old photos to be saved or disposed of. Old photos from Uni days, including wedding photos – not expensive photos to be framed and displayed, but cheap, candid shots taken by friends at the Registry Office. Her and Josh looking happy, goofing about, trying to look like a married couple who meant it to last, rather than doing it for a laugh. She had intended to create an album, or a Memory Box, but never got around to it. Now they could live in a shoe box under the bed until she decided what to do with them, or the faint dull ache in her heart finally faded to nothing.

Living together for three years at Uni had been fun, and maybe they should have left it at that? But they got married, stayed with his parents in Leeds for a few months, then moved down to a cheap little rented flat behind Golders Green Tube station. A neighbourhood pretentiously called Hampstead Garden Suburb. North of the river a different world; South East Londoners rarely cross the great divide. But it was OK, she liked it, and they were happy enough for a while, weren't they?

Ok, enough of this 'nostalgia ain't what it used to be' stuff. Time to concentrate on today and whatever horrors it might bring. Why the hell had she agreed to go to Ozzie's party, and, worse than that, to turn Animal into some semblance of a human being? She sincerely hoped that the fistful of notes Neil had given her to effect this miraculous transformation would be sufficient.

*

'I don't know why you're so off with me,' Animal complained. 'What have I done?' he was actually driving the van through a car wash at that moment and had to speak rather louder than usual over the foaming flip-flopping roller brushes swishing past the windows.

'Why couldn't you have done this before?' said Cass.

'We've got all day haven't we?'

'I'd rather get it over and done with as soon as possible.'

'It wasn't my idea to go clothes shopping – it was Neil's. But I thought we could at least have a nice time together. And some lunch. I'm getting peckish.'

'It's only half past eleven.'

'So? What about elevenses?'

'Get us out of this car wash and drive us to Lewisham Shopping Centre. I have a timetable for this morning, and we are not deviating from it or you will regret it.'

'Fuck me, you can be very scary, you know?'

'Oh, you have no idea how scary I can be,' said Cass, as they rolled out of the car wash tunnel in the whitest of old white vans.

*

'Shoes first, then some really plain boring trousers – maybe M&S, if they still have an M&S,' said Cass, dragging Animal out of the car park towards the shopping mall.

'M&S? I haven't been in there since I was a kid and my Mum bought me a school jumper,' he complained. 'Why can't I just wear my own trousers?'

'Have you got any decent trousers?'

'I've got another pair of jeans that I haven't even worn yet.'

'No. We are going for smart casual, I might just let you get away with some expensive looking cords, but no jeans. Right, in here – shoes, nothing too flashy, but something you'd like to wear.' She pushed him into the shoe shop and steered him past a rack of trainers, avoiding anything too brightly coloured. As she might have suspected his taste in footwear was not great, but with a bit of persuasion he settled on a pair of reasonably passable size elevens. Dark tan leather, a bit more expensive than anticipated, but shoes were important. Wasn't it Liz Taylor who once said that you should spend most money on your shoes and your mattress as you spent half your life *in* one, and half your life *on* the other?

'Are they comfortable? Walk up and down in them,' said Cass.

'God, you sound just like my Mum!' he grinned at her but obeyed. He seemed to be enjoying the shopping experience rather more than he should.

'Can we go for a coffee break yet?'

'No,' said Cass. 'Trousers first, then a coffee break.'

Trousers were a little more problematic – there was nothing suitable in M&S, where Animal looked longingly towards the café where several elderly ladies sat eating pastries and chatting over coffee. Once outside, Cass steered him towards the nearest man's shop and began to rifle through racks of trousers checking leg lengths.

'What's your inside leg?' she asked.

'You could measure it for me?'

'In your dreams! You're an extra-long, about 33 or 34?'

'I guess,' he shrugged. 'My waist is 34, I remember that. Or was it 36?'

'We'll find out when you start trying them on. Let's see what we've got here.'

Very few styles seemed to come in all the various permutations of short, regular, long. The basic rule seemed to be that the one you liked only came in the wrong length.

'Why are you such a ridiculous leg length?' Cass said.

'Sorry! Can't help being tall, can I? I like these ones,' he said, pointing out a pair of dark blue cords that were actually quite smart.

'Yes, and they'd come halfway up your calf,' Cass snapped. 'Look at the inside leg measurement. Oh, come on, we're going.'

'Where?'

'Back to the van. We're going to Greenwich market. We're going vintage.'

*

Once in the van Animal began complaining again about

missing a coffee break. 'And it's nearly lunch time too!'

'OK, we'll whizz through the shopping, have a late lunch, then you've got a hairdressing appointment at three.'

'What?'

'You didn't think you were going to turn up at Ozzie's party looking like – well, like you do? I've booked you in with my favourite guy – Franco. He's amazing. Wait and see.'

'You don't have to be so sarky with me, I'm doing this for you, aren't I?'

'We're doing this for Neil and Brian, remember?'

'Yeah, but I'm doing this for *you*. Cinderella shall go to the Ball! And you could be a bit nicer to me – after all, we shared a moment at that party, didn't we? We had a connection?'

'What?'

'At the wrap party – that night? When I came to your window? Don't tell me you didn't want company? I could see you did. You looked sad.'

'You're out of your mind. We never 'had a moment' we never 'had a connection'. That's the sort of thing they're always saying on daytime soaps!'

'You can tell when a woman wants you, it's in the pheromones. You can smell it.'

'Ugh! That's disgusting!'

'No it's not – it's science. It was on the medical programme with that woman doctor with the earrings like chandeliers?'

'Just drive and keep your eyes on the road. Forget about pheromones.'

But somewhere in the back of her mind was a horrible thought that if she were feeling vulnerable enough maybe even a hug from Animal would not be unwelcome? From now on it might be wiser to stay sober at parties. And Ozzie's party might at least provide a distraction from her gloomy bouts of nostalgia, or her regrets about Declan O'Neil.

*

Greenwich market was the answer. A vintage shop provided a sharp looking 1950s American jacket and a pair of dark chinos that looked the part. An upmarket menswear shop that prided itself on always being on trend provided a soft grey cotton shirt with a tiny horseshoe print that looked like a Ralph Lauren rip-off and cost more than they could afford but was so perfect that Animal actually produced a credit card and covered the cost. Late lunch turned out to be sandwiches and a coffee from Paul's Bakery consumed on the hoof as they trotted off to the hairdressers for three.

'Well, it's a challenge,' said Franco, a skinny boy with blonde curly hair and arms covered in tattoos, viewing Animal's hair and beard with a professional eye. You might have imagined a resemblance to one of the Muppets could have been the inspiration for his nickname if you didn't know better, thought Cass.

'What do you want me to do?' Franco asked her.

'I usually…' Animal began, but soon shut up as Cass and Franco started discussing him as if he were not there.

'OK, we can give it go!' said Franco. 'If you'd just come over to the basin?' and he wafted Animal into the rear of the shop to be shampooed, as Cass was led away to the front of the salon. Senior stylist Maria had time for a quick catch up over a shampoo and blow dry, and a complimentary cup of tea and biscuits. A trip to the hairdressers is better than psychotherapy any day, Cass thought to herself not for the first time.

About 45 minutes later Cass was good to go, and just paying at the front desk when she was joined by a Hipster with fashionably trimmed hair, moustache and beard, wearing a vintage 1950s American jacket over a soft grey print shirt and dark chinos. 'I just did a quick change in the Gents to give you the full effect,' the Hipster explained. 'What d'you think, Flash?'

'Scrubs up good, doesn't he?' said Franco, accepting a five-pound tip.

'Wow!' said Cass, momentarily lost for words. The Hipster spread out his arms to embrace her, but she sidestepped him and hugged the tattooed young stylist, planting a kiss on his cheek. 'You're a genius, Franco!'

Franco blushed and preened with pride.

'Why does he get a kiss and I don't?' grumbled the Hipster, as Cass pushed him towards the door.

'Because!' she said. Because Franco had transformed Animal into something that might not look totally out of place at Ozzie's party. The kind of gentrification that had turned an old Greenwich butcher's shop into a smart hairdressing salon with neatly trimmed hair on the floor instead of sawdust had worked its magic once again.

Chapter 20

Supermoon I

It was six o'clock on Friday evening already, and Alison was in no mood for complaints from the twins about not getting crispy fish fingers like the ones the Dinner Ladies served up at their school. She had to get the girls organised and out of the house in half an hour for their trip down to her mother's.

'Allie, can you fix these cuff links for me? The damn things never go right,' Ted was whining behind her back, as Alison tried to hurry the girls through their tea.

'Wait a minute, you're not wearing that shirt are you?' she said, swinging round with two plates of soggy fish finger rejects in her hands.

'What's wrong with it? It's my best shirt, isn't it?' Ted asked, losing the fight with his onyx cuff links.

For a moment Alison was tempted not to tell him that the shirt he'd chosen to wear with his tux was as lemon yellow as the anaemic homemade fish fingers she'd cooked for the kids. For all she cared he could turn up at a formal dinner wearing a yellow shirt and a red bow tie looking like Bozo the Clown. But, on the other hand, it might reflect badly on Declan, after all, this was his big *Psychiatry Today* presentation night and Ted was there as his support act, so she relented.

'Ted, you're colour blind – now go upstairs and put on the shirt I laid out on the chair for you to wear. And you won't need cuff links. Now scoot!'

'Oh, I didn't see it.'

'Because you don't look! You expect me to do everything for you! Well, please remember from now on everyone in this house is responsible for their own knickers and overcoats!' she said, scraping the leftovers in the compost caddy before dumping the plates in the sink. Ted could load the dishwasher later, after all, only *men* know how to load a dishwasher properly, don't they?

'Mummy's cross with Daddy,' Freya whispered gleefully to Sasha, and the twins took their chance to leave the table and sneak off to pack their own knickers and overcoats for the trip to Grandma's. Debbie followed in their wake, dragging a flight bag of assorted necessaries that she'd packed all by herself earlier in the day. It included several odd socks, a Peppa Pig T-shirt, a teddy bear, a bar of her favourite soap and an old toothbrush. (Her new plastic travel toothbrush in the shape of a shark had mysteriously disappeared and Alison had given up all hope of finding it before the next millennium, when it would probably turn up in some future archaeologist's trawl of unexplained historical artefacts. Probably a ritual object?)

Alison ran upstairs two at a time, pushing Ted ahead of her, and told him to sort himself out as she threw some overnight things into a suitcase for herself and the kids.

'I don't know why you're being so ratty,' said Ted. 'You're going to have a lovely weekend away at the seaside – I have to sit through Declan's speech, which is going to be either incredibly boring or incredibly embarrassing, or both. Whichever way you look at it you've got the better deal.'

'You know it means a lot to him, he's relying on you,' Alison said.

'I know, I know, I'm driving the gear up there for him, aren't I? After all, he can hardly turn up in the old Fun Bus, can he? I'll have to stay sober and probably end up driving him home too.'

'Just make sure you do stay sober. If I leave now, we should get there by nine, or nine thirty. I'll text you when we arrive.'

'Drive carefully. And give my regards to your mother,' Ted added, checking his appearance in the bedroom mirror. 'Will I do?'

'You'll do – hang on a minute, 'Alison ran to pick up a tiny gold safety pin from her dressing table and fixed it to the inside of Ted's right hand jacket cuff. 'There you are – right hand: pin, left hand: no pin. Got it?'

'OK. Thanks,' he grinned. 'I'll remember. And I'll look after Declan, promise.'

'You better had – he's relying on you, even if you don't know your right from your left.' *Or your arse from your elbow,* she was tempted to add, quoting one of her dear old Nan's favourite sayings. He was truly hopeless and helpless without her, wasn't he?

'Mum! Where's my travel bands?' came Freya's voice from the twins' bedroom.

'Travel bands? We're not flying to Grandma's!' Alison objected.

'Give her the travel bands, said Ted. 'It will keep her happy and with any luck you won't have her throwing up over the back seat.' And he was probably right, so she went to root out the travel bands and finish packing.

Alison sometimes wondered if she was a Tiger Mama or a Turtle Mama? She'd listened to all the podcasts on bringing up daughters for success in later life, but still was not convinced she was getting it right. A Tiger Mama pushed, structured, encouraged, organised and guided her girls, whilst a broad backed Turtle Mama left them to find their own way to the wide ocean of life. There must surely be merit in both approaches?

Their own mother had definitely been a Turtle Mama, so why, left to their own devices, had they turned out so differently? Take Maths for instance: tutored by their accountant father on the rare occasions when he was around, Alison had taken to numbers like a duck to water – or was it a fish? – whereas to Cass they remained incomprehensible. Dyscalculia was her get-out. On the other hand, whenever they were on holiday whilst Mum, Dad and Alison struggled to decipher street signs with the aid of a basic phrase book, Cass absorbed languages by some kind of osmosis just as easily as she picked up unsuitable boyfriends – Franco, Juan, Jean-Yves, or once in Mexico even a Romeo. Shy, careful

Alison could only look on with a tinge of jealousy, checking the taverna reckoning for any minor inaccuracies, as Cass flirted with the locals in a plethora of dialects. Come to think of it, numbers were not that much fun after all.

Maybe it wasn't in your upbringing but all in the genes? Maybe you were born to be an accountant, or to have the gift of tongues? Born to be a success or a psychopath? She shuddered at the thought and waved it away. She found the travel bands at the back of Ted's sock drawer along with a half-eaten tube of blackcurrant throat sweets well past their sell-by date that had glued themselves to a pair of unused trainer socks. They'd never be missed. Ted lacked the sporty gene. She binned the socks along with the sweets.

*

Alison had loaded the twins into the car and placed Debbie, already in her pyjamas, into her seat. With any luck she'd sleep through most of the journey to her Grandma's. With a last few instructions to Ted, and a goodbye kiss, she was off. Forgotten anything? No, she didn't think so.

'Mum, can we have a story?' said Freya, the most easily bored of the girls. She usually elected herself their spokesperson.

'What would you like?' asked Alison.

'Witch on a Stick!' She meant *Room on the Broom* of course. This was the current favourite and Alison found the CD and turned it on for them. The previous CD was *Cosi fan Tutti* – Ted must have been listening to that the last time he borrowed her car. Alison didn't mind a bit of Mozart herself, but Ted was the real opera buff. He'd once made her listen to the whole of Benjamin Britain's *Peter Grimes* while he conducted with a baton. That had been back in their student days. It wouldn't happen now.

As she drove further out of London and down towards West Sussex the light began to fade, and a huge full moon rose over the countryside. What did they call it? A supermoon? There was a song about that, wasn't there? All three girls had all dozed off by now and she was able to switch off the story. They must know it by heart, she thought. Not too bad a journey, only two potty stops so far and one 'I feel sick' false alarm from Freya.

Alison was glad to be getting away from everything for at least a little while. There had been an arrest following Trudi's death, a thief known to the local police but with no previous record of violence. No connection to the so-called Deptford Wolf killings. Just one of those horrible chance happenings. If only Trudi had arrived home a few minutes later, if only they had gone for a coffee together after Playgroup that morning… But that was not the way things turned out. Instead the children had sent hand-picked flowers to a quiet family funeral and the toddlers, too young to really understand, had come home from Playgroup the following week with 'sad news' to tell their mothers, who already knew.

She switched on the car radio, searching for something classical or something country to keep her mind alert and away from gloomy thoughts. Failing that she could always pop *Così* back in the player – they'd once seen a lovely open-air production of *Cosi* at Garsington Opera. Another year they'd made the mistake of taking Cass along with them to see *The Marriage of Figaro* – Ted had been given complimentary tickets by some big drugs company or other. It was a magical production, beautiful to watch on a warm, soft summer evening, and it even had supertitles projected above the stage that only went wrong a couple of times, but Cass complained about massive holes in the plot and why, when a girl dressed-as-a-boy called Cherubino was hidden in the Countess's wardrobe, did the Count not just open the bloody wardrobe door, instead of the two of them singing at each other for at least ten minutes *'There's a man in your closet / Oh no there isn't / Oh yes there is'* ?

Alison settled on a station playing the Eagles *Hotel California* and relaxed. She had to admit that if it came to a choice between Mozart and the Eagles, she'd probably opt for the latter. Though there were some beautiful moments in opera – it wasn't all *Peter Grimes* grim – what was that one they'd seen the other year? *Der Rosenkavalier* – another one with a girl-dressed-as-a-boy, but that's all right, because it's opera, and boys can be girls, and the moment the handsome young Rosenkavalier, resplendent in shimmering silver, presents the rose is enchanting…

And suddenly, with a shiver, Alison thought once again of another single anonymous rose – the one that had turned out to be from Declan, when he was still Dexy and her first love. And how that rose had been brought to her door by a delivery man she'd never seen before and never saw again.

And how she'd opened the door to him and accepted the Valentine's Day red rose. A sweet romantic gesture. What could be more innocent than a man delivering a single blood red rose to your door – a helmeted courier on a motorbike, or ubiquitous white van man? Of course, you'd open your front door to him, wouldn't you? And that's how the so-called Deptford Wolf operated. She knew it for a fact but who would ever believe her?

She had phoned the local Police Liaison Officer and told them about her intuition and they had listened politely, patiently, and told her the call would be logged. And that was about as far as it would go. She was only Debbie's Mum, the Twins' Mum, nobody clever, nobody special, just another concerned caller. But she could always put out a warning on Mumsnet, couldn't she? So that's what she had done, much to the chagrin of every florist in the area as their trade in red roses dropped off the sales graph. But if it stopped someone answering the door to an unexpected Rosenkavalier it might just save another woman's life.

Chapter 21

Supermoon II

It was the end of the week and the end of the month, the day of the *Psychiatry Today* dinner, and Declan was not looking forward to it with relish. He'd taken to early morning swimming at the gym where he had a year's membership courtesy of Ted – an unexpected Christmas present, and for once a gift he welcomed. The little orange tree complete with miniature fruits sitting in a rustic pot they'd gifted him the previous year had been an awful responsibility, even if it did enhance the balcony of his bachelor flat. It liked a bit of sunshine during the day, but he'd lived in dread of a killer frost and diligently hauled it inside the lounge every night until the danger seemed safely past. Maybe the little orange tree had been Alison's idea. A kind thought, but he preferred Ted's gym with all its facilities – mostly wasted on overweight middle-aged businessmen, or platinum card members like Ted who never visited it again after that initial New Year's Day workout.

Swimming always cleared Declan's head and prepared him for the day. And this wasn't going to be a good day. As he dried off in the locker room he got a brief message that one of his patients, a young woman, had been taken into the main hospital after a failed suicide attempt last night. He dressed in a hurry and left his hair wet.

*

Declan arrived at the ward in the main hospital building in time to have a few words with Brenda, the night nurse, before she went off duty. Brenda was a woman of substantial build and solid character. She was the kind of glue that held the place together during the long, sleepless hours that patients learned to dread.

'Oh, it's nothing to worry about,' said Brenda, 'just a bit of attention seeking. They bring her in last night after they pump out her stomach, then she locks herself in the girls' bathroom and tries to jump out of the window. But I let myself in and catch her by her knicker elastic – good, strong, convent girl knicker elastic – and haul her back inside. She come and sit beside me for the rest of the night, with her head on my knee, poor thing. She says everyone knows what her problem is, but no one can help her. She'll be pleased to see you, Dr O'Neil.'

'Thank you, Brenda. I'm sure you looked after her as well as anyone could.'

'It's my job, Doctor,' she shrugged. 'Now let me take you into the day room and I'll bring her through to you.'

It gave Declan a few moments to consider what the hell had happened and why had he missed the signs? There must have been signs? Why hadn't he seen them?

Brenda returned with a pale, exhausted looking girl, whose lank, untidy hair still carried traces of vomit. She sat the girl down on one of the armchairs.

'Oh, Dr O'Neil,' said Annie, 'I'm sorry I've caused you all this trouble…'

'I'll make you a nice cup of tea before I go, you just sit yourself there,' said Brenda, ignoring Declan's protestations that her shift was over. There was no arguing with Brenda.

'Annie, what happened?' Declan asked gently. 'Why didn't you tell me you were at risk?'

'I don't know… it just came over me…' she sighed and looked down at the floor, shielding her face with one hand, unable to raise her eyes to the cruel daylight. 'What is it those others know? The secret? The secret of how to live? Why don't I know it?' Her voice was low and flat, as if all the emotion had been drained out of her.

'Annie why don't you ask for help when you need it? You don't always have to put on a brave face.'

'I'm a nurse,' she said with bitterness now, 'I should know how to deal with this…this *thing*… I thought the Day Centre therapy sessions would help, I thought I'd beaten it this time. But I can't go back to work like this… I'm so angry with myself …'

'Well, yes, that's one way of putting it, you might say that depression is anger turned inwards but it's not your fault. None of this is your fault. You're not to blame. Sometimes you just need a bit of extra help to get out of it – to re-boot the old brain and make things run smoothly again?'

'I'm not having ECT!' Annie said, jumping up out of the chair and backing towards the door. 'You can't make me!' She knew what was coming.

'Annie, I wouldn't recommend it if I didn't think it was necessary. It can make the changes happen more quickly – it can give you the lift you need right now.'

'Here's your tea,' said Brenda, appearing in the doorway behind Annie with a couple of mugs in her hand. She looked from Annie to Declan and back again, sizing up the situation. She pushed her way in, put the mugs down on the table, took Annie gently by the arm and guided her back to the armchair. She placed a mug of tea in the girl's hands. 'You listen to what Doctor says,' said Brenda, 'he only wants what's best for you.'

'As soon as you're feeling better you can come back to the Day Centre group,' Declan promised. 'You can spend as much time there as you need before you go back to work. And you *will* be well enough to go back to work soon enough. But you need that little bit of extra help now, don't you?'

Annie drank her tea in several slow gulps, with tears running down her face, she nodded slightly but said nothing. A kind of submission. A kind of resignation.

Declan smiled and told her that he'd see her again in a day or two, and he was sure things would look very different. He promised a trip to Richmond Park on the Fun Bus as soon as she was ready for a day out and saw a flicker of a smile almost cross her face. Maybe he was a fool, but on bad days he sometimes thought a walk in the park probably did as much good as any other treatment he could offer. Oh fuck, he needed to get through this day without any more dramas if he was going to survive the presentation dinner tonight. But

Annie would be OK. She would be OK, he promised himself. He wouldn't let her down again.

Brenda nodded to him, her arm still around the girl, and Declan took his cue to leave and make arrangements for Annie's treatment.

*

Back in his office Declan was surprised to see a tux complete with evening shirt hanging from a hook on his door. The hire firm must have delivered it. But no, Marge informed him with a frosty demeanour, she had been to collect it for him.

'Not in my job description,' she said, 'But at least you managed to go for your fitting – I could hardly do that for you, could I?'

Declan thanked her profusely and looked as contrite as he possibly could, and Marge said she only hoped he'd sorted out his shoes and socks and he assured her that he would, though of course he hadn't yet given it much thought, the way things were today. Marge gave him one of her looks but left him to get on with the rest of his day's workload.

*

That evening, socks sorted as promised, Declan paced up and down his lounge, practising his speech as he had so many times before, when the landline rang. Probably someone warning him about PPI or selling insurance. He answered it anyway, and heard a distant male voice saying *Help me*.

'Who is this?' said Declan. It could be prank, or it could be one of his private patients in distress. But the voice merely rasped again *Help me* – then the phone went dead. A bad line

– or a prank? Who knows, but tonight Declan had other things on his mind. He went to change into his hired evening suit and the least bad pair of black shoes he could muster.

Ted had agreed to take all his gear for him – his laptop, papers, laser pointer– while Declan intended taking the Tube into town. He didn't trust himself to carry his own equipment by rail or tube tonight. What if he left it on the Tube? A terrifying prospect – hadn't that happened to someone famous? Wasn't it T.E. Lawrence who'd left the one and only manuscript of *The Seven Pillars of Wisdom* on a train and had to rewrite the whole damn thing? Or was that the literary equivalent of an urban myth? Who knows? His mind was wandering again. Must focus, must keep a clear head tonight. Must not think about Cass and her wolf *tulpa* that could have knocked all his research into a cocked hat or been a game-changer for his career.

What if a thought really could take on a physical form? After all what were thoughts, but electrical impulses generated in the mind? What was a 'mind' anyway – let's not get metaphysical – if you could describe a mind as an electrical matrix created by a physical brain that could be rebooted by a shot of ECT? So, what if a specific set of electrical impulses could organise molecules and atoms into a living thought form? Now we're in the realms of speculative fiction or Victorian seances with fake ectoplasm! Declan dismissed these thoughts and struggled with a bow tie that didn't want to sit straight. He looked at himself in the mirror and decided it would have to do.

The landline rang again, and this time he ignored it. It was half past six already. Too late, mate, leave a message after the tone. But when a brief text pinged into his mobile, he couldn't ignore that. Missing the signs of Annie's growing distress had put her life at risk and he wasn't going to repeat that kind of mistake. This text was a cry for help that needed to be answered.

Declan called Ted immediately. 'I need you to do me a favour, 'he said, 'I have to go somewhere before the dinner, if I'm a bit late can you set up the gear and stall them for me?

'What?' came Ted's voice. 'Where've you got to go? Do you need me to come and pick you up?'

'No. We'll meet at the dinner as planned. But I might be delayed. I have to go and see a patient.'

'Oh, you are *joking*! This is no time to be making house calls.'

'It won't take long – see you later! But if the worst comes to the worst, and it won't, you can always give the talk for me. You know my stuff every bit as well as I do, you've said so yourself,' and he ended the call before Ted could complain more than muttering 'you owe me'. And hoped to God that this particular house call wouldn't take that long.

Chapter 22

Supermoon III

It was the end of the week, the night of Ozzie's party, and Cass was not looking forward to it with any great enthusiasm. By six o'clock she was running a bath, ignoring the usual complaining noises from the boiler and pipework, tying up her hair, and wondering if there was any way she could bale out at this late stage? OK, Neil and his partner Brian were expecting her to go and schmooze along with them in hopes of hooking the new Afro products commercial, but surely they could manage without her? Apparently not.

The thought of having to accept another lift from Animal was not a happy one. Enough that she'd had to take him shopping but now she had to allow him to escort her to probably one of the most exclusive parties in Canary Wharf. Well, she hoped it was exclusive – exclusive enough to exclude her ex-husband. Not that she was keeping tabs on him, but his social media always showed him turning up in the all the right places looking like he almost belonged there. What was that classic Carly Simon song? *You're so vain?* It might have been written about Josh Green.

Animal messaged her for about the fifth time that evening with selfies of his new outfit. He looked very pleased with himself. Cass shuddered and turned her phone to silent. A pity she couldn't block him. Oh God this evening was beyond the call of duty! But, on the other hand, Ozzie was gorgeous and, no doubt, a good host, and certainly a contact worth cultivating. All this ran through her mind as she laid out her little black dress and beautiful pre-loved stilettos on the bed, then slipped in and out of the hot bath for a mere ten minutes. Steam was good for the skin, but not too much steam, and time was running on. The boiler and the pipework were still making complaining noises from somewhere overhead, and Cass made a mental note to summon the plumber back to take another look at the heating system.

Sitting in front of the mirror to apply anti-aging serum and moisturiser in the right balance took less time now that the little Makeup Girl had instructed her in the dark arts of cosmetics for her skin type. And, of course, the right kind of foundation correctly applied took five years off your age. As she performed this minor miracle, in the background a small TV was churning out the news, something about a cougar escaping from a zoo in Seattle and killing five other animals before it was brought down by a marksman with a tranquillizer gun. The big cat had not eaten any of the animals it killed, merely dispatching them swiftly and efficiently in a bid to establish its own territory. That was its nature, the zoo keeper explained when interviewed. All very well, thought Cass, but tough on the other poor beasts, including a random kangaroo and a wallaby. They had certainly come a long way from home to meet with sudden death.

As she slipped on the black dress, aware that Animal would be here any minute, Cass heard the front door opening and closing noisily. It made her jump.

'Only me, Mrs Green,' came the cheerful voice of Mr Barycz, 'just dropped by with my bill and your spare keys.'

'Oh, it's you. OK, leave them on the table, can you?' Cass called back. 'And can you take another look at the heating system as soon as possible? It's still making those weird noises. The radiators are knocking too.'

'Okey-dokey, I'll have to check my diary and let you know. Next week. Or soon as. Goodbye!' And with that the door opened and closed again behind him.

Cass put on the shoes that would probably cripple her by the end of the night and took a critical look at herself in the long mirror. It would have to do. The dress had come back from the dry cleaner's, where that nice woman had managed to get rid of some particularly difficult wine stains and warned her to avoid drinking red in future. It fitted like a glove and was the only thing in her wardrobe that suited the occasion – not too formal, not too casual, looking expensive but understated. Cass grabbed her bag and picked up her phone, just as the lights went out. For a moment she was blind, then with moonlight streaming in through her window, and the blue light from her phone, her eyes accustomed themselves to the semi-darkness.

Reflected in the long mirror was the figure of a chunky

looking man silhouetted in the doorway.

'Mr Barycz? Is that you? There's been a power cut.' Cass swung around, using her phone as a torch. The man's face was muffled with a black scarf around the mouth, and he wore a woollen hat pulled down over his brow. In one hand she saw what looked like a knife. Something told her this wasn't a local jewellery thief.

Cass moved rapidly, slamming the bedroom door in his face, with little hope of it holding very long as he pushed his weight against it. This was not looking good. She texted a brief message to the only person she could think of who'd come without question and was still texting when the door gave way and the man pushed his way into the bedroom. Cass leapt onto the bed and seized a bedside lamp and lobbed it at him, but it fell short, pulled back by the flex. She made a grab for a small travel bag on her bedside table and threw that at the figure, screaming at him to get out in fear and sudden anger. But he was too close, too quick, reaching out for her, and Cass began to really regret killing off her dream-wolf. Now would have been a very good time to have a real-life imaginary friend at your side. But she had destroyed her wolf *tulpa*, hadn't she? How unfortunate! What she needed now was something even bigger, stronger, fiercer – something that killed at will without conscience or compunction. Something feline? A Surrey puma or a Seattle cougar would do very nicely. And she needed it quickly.

*

Declan found himself in a taxi with a dour and unusually

silent driver. Declan looked at the brief message on his phone again – *Help me! Carnivore* – predictive text for *Carnival Street?* Cass was in distress, and he hoped it wasn't too late to offer her whatever support she needed. He wasn't going to fail her, if she was at risk of self-harming.

'Can't we go any faster?' said Declan.

'You got to watch the potholes along here, mate, don't want to ruin my suspension,' grumbled the driver. But he speeded up a little as they came down the hill towards Greenwich. Carnival Street was moments away. Declan pointed out Cass's flat and asked the driver to wait.

'Can't do that along here, mate, it's all permits. Just ring for another when you're ready,' he said, pulling up behind a white van that either had a permit, or whose owner took his chances.

Declan leapt out and paid the driver. It was barely more than twenty minutes since he'd got Cass's text. He'd tried ringing her several times, but no luck. He rang the doorbell of her flat, but no reply. There were no lights on inside – maybe she wasn't here? Maybe she'd gone walkabout? He guessed there was a back door to her flat, so he ducked down the little alleyway between the old houses, and found himself at the rear of the building, where a man was climbing up on a dustbin to peer in at a window set fairly high in the wall. It was a smallish window propped open on a metal catch for fresh air.

'Hey! What's going on?' Declan called.

'Who are you?' said the man, turning around to stare. He didn't look like your average burglar, more like a Hipster on a night out.

'I'm Mrs Green's doctor, this is her flat. Who are you?'

'I'm her date, if it's any of your business. I've been trying to get her to answer the door – but …' There was a genuine note of concern in the young man's voice.

'Have you been here long?' asked Declan.

'Couple of minutes. But she knew I'd be over to pick her up – something's not right.'

'She asked me to come over, it sounded urgent.'

'Listen! I can hear something going on inside. God, what was that?'

'Can you get in through that window?' asked Declan.

'Give us a leg up,' said the man, 'I can squeeze through – I think.'

With Declan pushing and supporting him, the man managed to climb up onto the window sill. The window was made of bobbled glass in a wooden frame that lifted up vertically on a hinge. The man pushed it up as high as it would go with his arm and pulled one leg up to the windowsill and swung it over. With a bit more effort he managed to slide his body in through the narrow opening. He dropped out of sight and Declan heard a loud splash and some even louder cursing.

'What's happening?' shouted Declan. 'Is Cass there?'

'Aw, fuck – I've landed in a bath full of water. Ok, I'll go an' open the back door.' And the voice faded away.

As Declan waited impatiently, he tried phoning Cass again. Still no reply. When the back door finally opened, Declan pushed in past the man, and hurried into the flat, calling Cass's name. He went into the bedroom, a complete mess, lit only by moonlight. But no sign of Cass, just a tumble of bedclothes on the floor, and things scattered around at random.

'Where's the light switch?' Declan called.

'Lights are off,' said the man, following him down the hall. 'I've already tried. Fuses must have tripped out when the pipes started leaking.'

'What's leaking?' said Declan, pushing open the lounge door.

'There's water coming through the bathroom ceiling,' said the man, 'I'm fucking soaked. You need to go and find the stopcock. Turn it off at the mains.'

'I'm a psychiatrist, not a plumber!'

'What? Oh, I'll do it – you look for Cass!' said the man and turned back, as Declan groped his way to the lounge by the light of his phone. The lounge was a long room, with a sofa at one end, mostly in shadow. Declan could make out a person lying on the sofa, a woman, and over her crouched the shape of a big cat. Moonlight from the large bay window at the far end of the room gave the scene a strange, unreal glow.

Declan froze for a moment, not knowing what to do. But the beast heard – or smelled him – and turned to look at him with steady green-gold eyes. And as the puma, or whatever the hell it was, stared at him, the shape of the woman became a misty wraith, fading into the shadows. Nothing left but a pile of clothes and a shoe that clattered to the floor. The puma began to unpeel itself from the spot where the woman had been and stretched its limbs. It was solid and real enough, wherever it had come from. Declan slowly backed away. But maybe that was the wrong thing to do, maybe you were supposed to stand still and stare it out? God knows!

From the corner of his eye he noticed that the ceiling directly above the sofa in the bay window was beginning to belly and sag in a most alarming way. There was a groaning and wheezing noise from the pipework above, and Declan guessed that the stopcock had not yet been located. There was a drip of water from the centre of the bulge above the sofa. It surely wouldn't hold under the strain much longer – and it didn't. The bellying ceiling gave way under the weight, showering the puma with a gush of hot water.

The puma leapt up like the proverbial scalded cat and flung itself through the bay window, shattering the glass as it went. The puma ran out into the street, heading up the hill towards the park and the heath, and it only took a moment for Declan to decide to follow it.

Chapter 23

Astral Festival

It was the first night of the Greenwich Astral Festival, a celebration of astronomy timed to coincide with the supermoon, hosted by the Observatory. People were making their way up through Greenwich Park carrying little candles in paper holders that would be safely extinguished at the top of the path, as they reached the location for tonight's live edition of *Skywatching* with Professor Brian Cox and several minor celebs. It was a pretty sight to see the column of star gazers making their way up the park towards General Wolfe's statue and beyond. And it was a piece of bad luck that it had to be tonight of all nights, thought Declan as he dodged his way up the grassy slopes, sometimes mingling with the crowd, sometimes darting off to the side when he thought he glimpsed something running through the trees.

He had been chasing shadows for a good while now, running as hard as he could along Crooms Hill, into the park via Circus Gate, following his instincts rather than any real sighting of the puma. Every now and then there was a glimpse of a cat shape, a flicker of a long tail, a swift movement that drew him onwards. If somehow Cass had created the puma, then swapped places with it, then he had to find her or her puma avatar. However crazy it sounded, he couldn't come up with another explanation for what he'd witnessed.

His chest was hurting as he flung himself back onto the path and began panting up the hilly slopes. He tripped and crashed into a lanky young man wearing a Metallica T-shirt and holding a candle in one hand. He grabbed Declan by the arm and helped him right himself.

'Steady mate! You all right?' he said.

Declan could only puff and nod, resting his hands on his thighs and catching his breath for a moment or two. He was winded. The lanky man went on his way up to the Observatory, where the spectators were gathering.

Declan began to think he must be a complete idiot. He should have called out the police, or fire Brigade, or done something, instead of leaving it to that so-called date of Cass's back at the flat. The Fire Brigade must be experienced in dealing with big cats on the loose? You'd imagine so, wouldn't you? It must have started happening in the 1970s, when the law on keeping exotic animals came into force, and some of those 'pets' were set free?

By now he'd nearly reached the top of the park, avoiding the crowd gathering around the Observatory to see Professor Brian Cox, and paused to look around in hopes of catching sight of the puma/Cass or Cass/puma. Nothing. Declan stopped, looked towards the open Heath, lit by the beams of the supermoon, wondering what to do next. Behind him he could hear music playing – something about a *pink moon* – that was Nick Drake, wasn't it? A talented young musician who'd been badly let down by the mental health services. At least his music lived on, perhaps giving him a kind of immortality.

The pain in his chest and the metallic taste of blood in his mouth was subsiding as he took a few slow, deep breaths. Behind him the Observatory crowd seemed to be getting excited – must be the imminent appearance of Brian Cox that had whipped them up into screaming? Oh Christ, no! They weren't screams of adulation for the science superstar but cries of panic.

Declan swung round and saw the assembled Festival goers beginning to scatter across the park – and in the midst of them, dancing in the bright moonlight, a large brown cat with a long tail. It leapt and twisted in the air, drawing away from the candles surrounding it, thrown to the ground in panic, and then streaked off up towards the Heath. It passed so close by Declan that he could feel the rush of air.

'Here we go again!' He began to run up towards the Heath following the animal wherever it led. There was something primeval in the chase, invigorating –- but he wished to God he'd worn his comfortable old trainers…

*

It was only a few minutes later when he found himself cornered by the puma in the little stone church on the top of the Heath that Declan realised he had absolutely no idea what to do. He had chased the big cat across the Heath, avoiding the odd dog walker or startled cyclist, and followed it to the church. The side entrance must have been left open by mistake, no one left churches open these days, did they? But he pushed his way into the building, following the dark shape that had slipped through the doorway before him.

The interior was dimly lit by moonlight shining through the stained-glass windows. As his eyes accustomed to the gloom, he could pick out the shapes of pews and the main aisle leading up to the altar. Not many places for a big cat to hide. Not really. He thought he could hear the slow padding sound of an animal somewhere nearby – was it imagination, or the beating of his own heart?

'Cass? Is that – is that you?' A ridiculous question, Cass was long gone. What was staring at him now with greeny-golden eyes was a puma. It slid out of the darkness to confront him silently.

'Cass – is it you in there somewhere, isn't it?' He began backing away slowly, never taking his eyes off the beast.

'Cass, please come back to me – I know you can hear me – you can trust me – because I care about you …I want to help.'

The puma paused for a moment.

'I'm sorry I didn't believe you – I understand now, you've created this *tulpa* thing and it's sucking the life out of you – OK, I get it – but you can fight back.'

By now the puma had Declan backed up against the choir stalls. It was making low snarling – or was it purring? – noises.

'An hour ago you were a woman – now you're – you're whatever you've become – but if you can pull a stunt like that once, you can do it again. You can reverse it, Cass. Come back!'

He stepped away from the choir stall, stumbling, leaning against the stone wall as the puma loomed over him. The big cat reached out a paw and cuffed his face – playfully or curiously? The effect was the same, Declan's head snapped back, and he almost knocked himself out against the wall. His eyes closed and he felt sick. Then nothing.

*

A long, quiet moment of nothing, then when he opened his eyes again the puma was gone. He pulled himself up into a sitting position in time to see a woman's naked arm reaching up from behind the choir stalls to grab one of the chorister's gowns hanging on the pegs above.

Sitting against the cold stone wall of the church, Declan began to feel he was in some kind of altered state. A woman stepped out from behind the choir stalls, tying the loose robe around her body. Her eyes were still the greeny-gold eyes of a puma, but the woman was undoubtedly Cass.

'What took you so long, Dr O'Neil?' she said.

'What?'

'To tell me you cared for me?'

'Cass!' he said and hugged her close, with a sense of relief. 'Please don't ever do this again? I don't think my heart could stand it.'

Back at Declan's flat after a silent taxi ride home, he checked her over for injuries. But apart from a couple of superficial grazes, Cass seemed remarkably healthy. He, however, was bruised about the face and would have a black eye by the morning. The hired evening suit had come off worst, with a splattering of mud and a good few rips and tears.

'Why are you wearing a tux?' asked Cass, over a mug of tea and a cheese sandwich. Transmogrification makes a girl hungry, as she said. Declan didn't even bother to ask what 'transmogrification' meant.

'I was on my way to give a presentation at a dinner this evening. It doesn't matter. There's always another dinner, another paper, another year.'

'I'm sorry I spoiled your dinner.'

'Don't be. You needed help.'

'And you came. Without question. That's quite something. Thank you. Now, I need to go home and get some clothes.'

'Cass, you can't go home, apart from the fact that you're probably still in shock, your home is a crime scene. You won't be allowed back until it's been processed – we should phone the police now.'

'I'm not talking to the police tonight! I can't, not yet, it's all scrambled in my brain. Nothing seems real.'

'That's hardly surprising. I'll ring and tell them that you're OK, and that you're staying with friends.'

'Yes. Staying with friends… With you?'

'If that's what you'd like, otherwise I can take you wherever you want.'

'I'd rather stay here, if you don't mind. I feel safe with you.'

'Safe? After what happened tonight I'm not totally sure *I* feel safe with *you*,' he said and he took her in his arms, just as he had in the little church on the Heath and held her close.

'I can't absolutely promise that it won't ever happen again,' she sighed and rested her head against his chest for a moment. 'I don't seem to be totally in control of it.'

'Then I suppose I'll have to take my chances,' he said. 'You can stay here.'

Cass reached up and kissed him gently on his bruised cheek. 'Did I do that?' she asked, looking up at him.

'Yes, your puma-avatar was a bit tactile.'

'I'm sorry.' Then she kissed him again on the mouth. And there was still a faint feline scent of musk about her that was not entirely unattractive.

'Cass – I'm not sure this is a good idea,' he said, pulling back.

'Why? Would you get struck off for something like this? I'm not your patient anymore, am I?'

'No, but it's something of a grey area – I still have a duty of care. A responsibility.'

She drew him back into her arms. 'Dexy, Dexy, please stop talking like a doctor. Let's just be you and me?'

'If that's what you want,' he said. 'I have a spare toothbrush for unexpected guests.'

'Do you have many unexpected guests?'

'To be truthful, you're the first in a while,' he said and led her to the bedroom.

'Good,' said Cass and closed the door behind them.

'Cass?' he asked, as she unbuttoned his shirt.

'What?'

'You're not going to um... *transmogrify* again any time soon?'

'Wouldn't dream of it!' she said and kissed him on the neck, gently nipping him with her sharp teeth.

Chapter 24

The Tanya

When Cass woke up on the chilly stone floor of that little church on the Heath her first thought had been *Where am I?* Her second thought was *Where the hell are my clothes?*

The events of the night seemed hazy, like a bad dream – or to be honest, like one of Neil's really bad horror movies. There had been a struggle with a man in her flat, that much she was sure of, a fight that she was losing, until she poured all her energy into something beyond her. A *tulpa* – that must have been it – but then her memories became confused. There was running and chasing – chasing something or being chased *by* something – and a sense of joy and freedom and power that she'd never experienced before... and then a voice calling her back from all the wonderful places she'd been in her mind, back to a cold, mundane world. And the practical need to find something to cover her nakedness.

'Is that really all you can remember?' asked Declan, handing her a mug of hot chocolate. They were sitting in the kitchen of his bijou apartment, rather more upmarket that might be expected of a man who bought his clothes from charity shops. There was even a miniature orange tree on the balcony. Cass had noticed it as he carried her in last night. He really didn't need to carry her, she was fine on her own two feet, but it was rather sweet.

'Yes,' said Cass. 'The man who attacked me must have switched off all the lights – or maybe it was a power cut. I only know it was dark…'

'It was most likely the earth tripped out, there was a leak in the ceiling – must have shorted out the electrics. Go on.'

'Oh, I can't really describe him other than short and chunky – he must have slipped in after Mr Barycz left. Maybe Barycz didn't shut the front door properly? I don't know. The man's face was half covered with a scarf; I can remember that much. And something else – I think my *tulpa* cat scratched him on the face before he ran away. But I can't be sure, because that's when it all went a bit strange.'

'A bit strange? Cass you turned into a – a puma or cougar, or whatever it was. I'd say that was *very* strange.'

'A puma, or a cougar – I think it's the same thing, isn't it? And I didn't turn into one. It was a *tulpa* – I created it, but it was too strong for me to control. It *changed places* with me for a while. But here I am, back again!' She smiled at him. But Declan was not smiling. He looked serious.

'There has to be an explanation for all this, some kind of scientific rational explanation. Maybe it's a whole new area of physics – things can't change into other things, like the old alchemists imagined.'

'Sir Isaac Newton thought they could,' she said. 'He was

into alchemy – he believed in the elixir of life and the philosopher's stone and all that stuff.'

'Well, he was a bit of an eccentric, wasn't he? But perhaps there is some kind of connection between you and the *tulpa* that allows this sort of thing to happen – like quantum entanglement, where things once in contact continue to interact at a distance – but that's at the subatomic level of quantum physics.'

'Ha! That's the First Law of Sympathetic Magic,' Cass laughed. '*Things once in contact continue to interact at a distance.* In my Goth phase I used to read a lot about magic – black magic, white magic, green magic.'

'This isn't getting us anywhere, Cass, we have to get our story straight for the police. I'm sorry about your friend getting himself arrested last night.'

'Oh, Animal will be OK, though why he had to go and call out the police and the fire brigade I don't know. We can confirm his story, that there was a break-in, and I was attacked, and the man ran away – that much is true. But we can be economical with the truth, can't we?'

'I don't think they'd believe it anyway,' he said. 'Come on, we need to get you some clothes from the boutique downstairs. You can't keep wearing my bathrobe.'

'It looks OK, it's a kimono, but your flipflops are a bit big for me,' said Cass, getting up from the breakfast table. 'For a man who buys all his clothes from charity shops, how do you afford living in an apartment block like this? If you don't mind me asking?'

'Bank of Mum and Dad and an unexpected legacy from one of my old Irish aunties. I put it into an 'executive starter flat'. But everything inside is pre-loved – like me,' he added ruefully.

'She really did break your heart, didn't she?'

'She did. But broken hearts – like broken minds – can be healed, given time. Shall we go?'

Cass flip-flopped out of the door and followed him to the lift. As they were going down to the ground floor, Declan's phone rang. He made a face at Cass. 'It's Ted. I could do without this now.'

'You've got to speak to him sometime, just be vague,' she said.

Declared answered the call and was genuinely as vague as possible about why he had not turned up to give his presentation at the *Psychiatry Today* dinner the night before.

'Don't worry,' came Ted's voice, 'it went down a storm – I gave the talk for you. Christ, we'd run through it enough times together, I knew the whole spiel by heart. They loved Wolfman and Rabbit Boy – oh, sorry, I wasn't supposed to mention him, was I? They lapped it up, even old man Frawley was in stitches.'

'Really? Well, I'm thinking of shelving the project for the moment.'

'Good man, then you can come into the 'me too' drug trials with Blonde – I'll set you up a meeting with them.'

'No thanks, Ted, definitely not interested in the drug trials. I have a few other irons in the fire. Speak to you soon.' And with that he ended the call.

'Irons in the fire?' said Cass.

'Oh yes. I'd say so. Now, let's get you some clothes, then nip down to the police station and make our statements. There might be some forensic evidence at your place that could give them a lead to this Deptford Wolf character.'

'You believe that's who attacked me? There was no red rose?'

'I don't know, but it's full moon, red rose or no red rose. And you said he had a knife?'

Cass shuddered. 'Yes, I remember thinking *that's a knife*, and wishing I hadn't killed off my wolf so quickly.'

'And your puma?'

'Oh, that was only ever a temporary expedient – a bit of leftover Goth magic? I was desperate, I needed something that could kill without conscience. It's gone now.'

'I hope you're right, Cass,' said Declan. 'I only hope you're right.'

*

He'd missed his early morning swim on Monday but managed to dash into the hospital for an hour or two before he was due to keep his appointment with Dr Weiss.

Marge seemed surprised to see him turn up at all. She was entering patient lists into the system and paused to give him a good look up and down.

'I thought you'd be keeping a low profile after failing to show up at that do on Friday night,' she said as he walked in, carrying the hire suit carefully zipped into the travel bag. He hoped she wouldn't feel the need to inspect it too closely before returning it for him by the end of the day.

'How d'you know about that?'

'Bush telegraph,' said Marge. 'Don't expect to keep any secrets here. And what do you want me to do with *that?*' she indicated the suit bag with a turn of her head.

'Ah, Marge, I wouldn't ask, but if you could drop it by the shop for me? And let them know I'll pay for any damage or extra cleaning. Just send me the bill?'

'Damage? Now I really want to know what you got up to on Friday night! Hang it on the back of the door. Have you go the hire ticket?'

'It's in the top jacket pocket,' he promised. 'Marge, you're a star. I'm going to be here a couple of hours, then I want to check up on Annie, one of the girls from my Day Centre Group who was admitted last week for ECT.'

'I think there's a message about that for you – it's all good, they're going to discharge her. You'll can pop over and see her now. I'll re-organise your diary, there only some pharmaceutical rep giving you a talk over lunch. You can give that a miss, can't you? But can you be back here at five sharp, as Dr Heaney want to catch up with you before he leaves?'

'Once again, you are a star, Marge,' said Declan, heading for the door.

'And Dr O'Neil, before you do show your face around here again, I suggest you get your story straight for Frawley, and perhaps wait until that black eye has completely gone? Whatever you were up to on Friday night, I hope the other fellow came off worse.'

*

Once he had seen Annie and agreed to her discharge, Declan drove over to Dr Weiss's house in the suburbs. He found himself pacing up and down in the study, with its rows of books and a coffee table bearing tea and today some little fairy cakes for two. Weiss was the only person he could trust with the truth about Cass, the puma, and himself. The whole improbable tale came tumbling out, sounding just as crazy to himself as it must to his elderly mentor.

'You have to admit, it's a hard story to swallow.'

'I hardly believe it myself,' said Declan.

'You don't think you are becoming too involved?'

'*Folie a deux?* That old chestnut?' A shared delusion?'

'No, actually I wondered if you were falling in love with the lady – or the tiger. Sorry. Not a tiger, a puma. Or a cougar? I've been your analyst long enough to know when you are not telling me the full story.'

'Yes, we're close – becoming closer – but that's not the thing. She creates these *tulpa* thought-forms that can take on a life of their own, if only for a limited time. I can't explain it, can't understand it, but I've seen it with my own eyes. And felt it too.' He gently rubbed his bruised cheek and shook his head.

'Perhaps I can help you understand,' said Dr Weiss and went over to the bookshelves that lined half the room and pulled out an old leather-bound book.

'This is the Likkutei Amarin, the *Tanya*,' he said. 'Didn't I tell you about it before? It deals with spirituality, psychology and theology. Let's see what Rabbi Schneu Zalman has to say about the dual nature of the human soul.'

'Yes, you told me, but I can't see what Hasidic mysticism has to do with a woman who can conjure up wolves, or turns into a big cat when she gets scared and angry?'

'Try thinking about the human soul as *two* souls – half animal, half divine. One draws us down towards the earth, the other draws us upwards – I'm sure the poet William Blake said much the same thing, didn't he? But what if the animal soul prevails? What then?'

Declan shook his head again and made a gesture with his hand to dismiss the idea.

'Why do you reject your cultural heritage?' asked Weiss.

'Which one? My dad's or my mother's? As a boy I sang in two choirs –*shul* on Saturdays, St Joseph's on Sundays.'

'And made good money singing at wedding, christenings and bar mitzvahs?'

'Yes, that's true,' Declan laughed. 'I was on to a good thing in the old boy soprano days. Pity my voice broke when it did, or I'd be a rich man by now.'

'But this is no laughing matter for the young lady. If what you say is true, then her immortal soul is in danger. Has she – the beast – has it killed yet?'

'No, good grief, no. The man who attacked her was scared off by the puma. Maybe it scratched him, but it certainly didn't kill him. That bastard's still out there.'

'But it's only a matter of time. You said she wanted to create something that killed at will without conscience? What happens if she finds herself in danger again?'

'But I thought we'd stopped all that when she came back to me? The puma's gone.'

'No, you have merely lulled it to sleep. Each time she creates one of these imaginary things – a *tulpa* – it becomes stronger, more dangerous. This time it was only able to change places with her for a short while, but once it kills and the animal soul becomes dominant, then, I am afraid, the change will become permanent. I am hazarding a guess that it would take some kind of emotional or physical crisis to integrate the animal and the human soul into balance again.'

'I'm not sure I believe in 'souls', or gods, or anything much anymore,' said Declan. He'd had more than enough religious instruction in his early life to last him. It hadn't turned him into a complete atheist though, just a confused agnostic with more pressing concerns to think about.

'Then accept it as a useful metaphor,' said Dr Weiss. 'Now, won't you have a cup of tea and one of these little cakes my wife has made?'

'Thank you. I can always make time for cake.'

'And Declan, your cat woman? Be careful: "The female of the species is more deadly than the male" you know?'

'Rabbi Schneu Zalman?'

'Rudyard Kipling!' He shook his head, what did they teach them at school these days?

Chapter 25

White Van Man

Saturday, Sunday, Monday had been long enough for Cass to begin to feel quite at home in Declan's flat. The interview with the police had not gone too badly, they seemed to accept her account of fleeing from an intruder and being taken home by Dr O'Neil to recover. Animal had corroborated her story. Though initially arrested as a person of interest – an unfortunate mistake – soon enough he'd be basking in the limelight of local hero as the man who had chased off the Deptford Wolf. She would have put money on it and was happy enough for that version of events to go viral.

The police were not officially commenting on whether it was or wasn't a Deptford Wolf attack, but the media were sure. *Supermoon Werewolf Killer Strikes Again* – you could see the headlines now. Cass wanted to stay well away from that, so it looked like she'd remain at her 'secret address' for a while. It perhaps wasn't quite the way she'd imagined getting together with the man of her dreams back in her teenage Goth days, but not far off, to be honest. She'd always had a rather macabre imagination, according to her English teacher.

But staying away from all her stuff was becoming

problematic. She felt lost without credit cards, bag, and phone – her whole life was in that phone. And knickers, a girl needs her own knickers. And shoes. The flat had been secured and broken window boarded up, the water had been turned off, but there was no knowing how much damage had been done until she could see it for herself. If her poor duvet had been soaked through all over again she would cry. By now, she hoped, the odd newspaper reporter would have given up and gone home. Surely it was safe to nip down and pick up a few clothes, her laptop and phone? She had promised Declan she'd wait for him to go with her, but by Monday afternoon the temptation was becoming too much. He'd left her some cash, she could take a taxi, be in and out of the flat using the spare key hidden behind that loose brick. She could throw a few things into an overnight bag and be back again within a couple of hours – three hours tops. No problem.

She was picking up her coat when the doorbell rang. Maybe Declan had forgotten his keys? Or a delivery to be signed for? But when she opened the door it was neither of these. It was a short, stocky man with a balding head, looking at a small yellow card grasped in his hand.

'Dr Declan O'Neil lives here?' he said, reading out the name on the card. 'You can help me?'

Cass gasped a tiny sound of surprise and the man looked up. As he turned his eyes towards her, she could see three long, deep, red marks clawed down the left side of his face. They looked like the claw marks of a large cat, barely healed.

'Mr Barycz !' she said, stepping back and trying to shut the door on him, but he lunged forward, dropping the little yellow card, grabbed her head in one large hand and slammed it hard against the door frame. Cass felt her knees give way as he dragged her, half stunned, out of the flat and pulled her towards the staircase. His other hand was over her mouth, stifling any attempt to scream or call for help as he dragged her down two flights of stairs to the underground car park. There was no one there to see him pull her over to a dirty white van, open the back doors, and push her inside with another fierce blow to the head that knocked her out.

*

When Cass came round she found herself in the back of a builder's van, amongst an assortment of plumbing equipment, paint pots, ropes, plastic buckets and tool boxes. It smelled of a strange chemical blend of everything that had ever travelled in there, and the jolting motion told her they were driving over potholed roads at some speed. Her hands were bound with something behind her back, and there was a strip of duct tape over her mouth. She felt nauseous and struggled to breathe properly, anxiety tightening her chest. Getting free of her bonds was not an option, but she managed to pull herself up onto her knees and tried to wriggle towards the back doors – even if she could open them, she could hardly throw herself out onto the road, could she? Rolling out in front of oncoming traffic? You could kill yourself!

She began to feel wobbly, her head still ringing. Her eyelids flickered and she fought to stay conscious, but just as she began to slip away again, she caught sight of something crouching in the corner of the van. It was misty and indistinct, something like a puma, something like a lynx, a wonky wild cat scribbled by a child's wax crayon. Or created by a desperate mind that needed all the help it could get to stay alive. As the wild cat became more and more solid, Cass felt herself drifting away, the bonds falling off, as her clothes became heavy and loose. Something else was taking her place. That much she knew before she lost consciousness again. Then she was gone.

*

Declan found Ted waiting for him in the hospital main reception, having returned from a business lunch presentation courtesy of a pharmaceutical 'rep' in the hospital's small education suite.

'Did I miss much?' Declan asked.

'No, just the usual plastic wrapped sandwiches and mineral water – honestly, why do they have to put mayo in everything these days? And houmous? I ask you, houmous in sandwiches. They've gone all soggy even before you open them. What happened to the good old bacon roll, or cheese and pickle sarnie of our Uni days?'

'You're a man of simple tastes.'

'I am, I am. Anyway, I'll make up for it tonight – Alison's cooking Boeuf Bourguignon with those little vegetable frites things – what?'

'I meant: did I miss anything worth noting from the rep's talk?'

'Oh,' Ted looked vague, but nodded. 'Maybe. I'll send you

the bullet points. Judge for yourself. Walk down to Jarrod's with me, then I'll give you a lift back home. I had a slow puncture this morning coming in, so I dropped the Porsche off at the garage before lunch.'

'OK, why not? I always walk in and out when the weather's like this.'

'Why don't you get yourself a decent car? You can afford it.'

'Parking? Congestion charge? Why would I need all that annoyance?'

'Point taken. But things change when you have a family to transport, believe me. Having children seems to involve an amazing amount of equipment, not to mention potty stops every journey.'

'Maybe one day the tables will be turned – you'll be the grumpy old guy with prostate issues, and they'll be ferrying *you* around making pub loo stops?' said Declan with a grin.

'God, what a thought! Come on, let's get a wriggle on.' And they kept a good pace down the hill, until Ted began to flag a little. But it didn't stop him launching into one of his pet topics. He was full of his latest scheme to get Declan a promotion, involving getting Frawley and the board caught in some kind of pincer movement.

'I can get it all set up – you don't want to spend the rest of your days driving a bunch of kleptomaniacs around in the Fun Bus, do you? But I guess you're not in the mood to discuss that now?' he said. 'Um…How is Cass?'

Declan had told him the bare minimum about Friday night and had no intention of filling in the blanks now. 'She's bearing up remarkably well. She'll be staying at mine for the time being.'

'You two getting along well? It's a very small place,' said Ted.

'Yes, we're together, if that's what Alison wants to know,' said Declan.

'Yes, well, sisterly concern. She wanted me to make sure that Cass is all right and that you're looking after her properly. She and the kids are staying down with her mother for a couple of days. Here we are, Jarrod's is just down there.'

To Declan's surprise they turned off into a small side street, at the end of which was a rather downmarket yard where several cars and a truck were parked. Ted led him to the little shed at the far end that served as an office, with *Jarrod & Sons* painted over the doorway.

'Not quite what you were expecting? Well, I'm not going to pay Porsche dealership rates for a simple job that the gnomes of Jarrod's can do at a fraction of a price.'

'Gnomes?'

'You'll see.' Ted opened the door and went into the waiting area, complete with a coffee machine and a TV screen mounted high on the wall, with a twenty-four-hour news programme running silently above them. Behind the desk a very elderly mechanic in traditional blue overalls, was taking a phone call. He waved to Ted and gave him a thumbs-up. The man was small, wizened, with a face full of wrinkles. He had a pallor that you sometimes see in men who spend much of their lives beneath the bonnets of cars.

'See what I mean?' said Ted. 'It's a gnome – or what's it, a troll? Oh, it's OK, he can't hear us – at least I don't think he can, there are two of them – twins – one of them's deaf. I think it's this one.' And at this point an identical gnome in blue overalls poked his head round the doorway and summoned Ted to collect his car.

Declan wondered what Ted would do when these old guys retired – he'd have to find himself another cut price garage. But that's how Ted held on to his money, wasn't it?

A rolling news item on the TV screen caught Declan's eye, and he saw a couple of shots of a panther or a jaguar, as the ribbon below announced '*Exotic big cats in the news again, with reports of a large brown cat with a long tail sighted in the Woolwich area of South East London…*' The silent news reader seemed amused at this item, and moved quickly on to the next, something about potholes. Declan wondered if they had been seen on the night of the puma. Or was this sighting more recent? Woolwich wasn't far.

As Ted came back in to settle the bill, Declan almost snatched the car keys out of his hand. 'Ted, lend me your car?'

'What?'

'Ted, it's an emergency, let me have the car for a while, will you?'

'Oh, Christ, not another one of your private patients – oh, shit, it's not Cass, is it?'

'It might be. It could be. I don't know.'

*

'Here, take the car, find her, she could be in delayed shock after all she's been through.' Ted pressed the keys into Declan's hands, and pushed him out of the door. 'And please take care of the Porsche!'

Chapter 26

Final Girl

The first heavy drops began falling as Declan raced out of the office shed and jumped into Ted's car, and there was that unmistakable scent of rain hitting the ground after a couple of dry summer days. Rivulets began to run down the windscreen as he moved out of the side road and down the hill, heading for Woolwich. It might be something, or it might be nothing, he thought, but there was a sick feeling in his gut.

He turned the radio to a local station that usually ran current stories with a touch of humour, or the bizarre. The announcer was midway through some item on stolen underwear from washing lines. The usual awful puns about knickers and nickers. So probably nothing to worry about. The announcer cut to a commercial, then came back with the next item:

'Now we've all heard those urban legends about the Surry Puma and the Beast of Bodmin, but if you keep your eyes peeled you might catch sight of something unusual in the Woolwich area today – we have reports coming in of sightings of a large cat-like creature down on the Woolwich Free Ferry. Apparently, the police are taking it seriously enough to send down a marksman – and a vet, of course. But if you ask me, it's probably just another shaggy dog story…'

Declan took the A102, A206 then into Church Street in record time. He may have been flashed by a speed camera back there, but he wasn't worrying about that. A call from Ted came up on the hands-free, wanting to know where he was and what was happening? Declan muttered something about calling him back as soon as he knew. He had tried calling Cass, but there was no answer from either the landline at his flat or from her mobile (just in case she'd been tempted to go and retrieve it against his advice).

There was a queue of cars backing up Ferry Approach, where at the far end Declan could see a police car with a couple of officers standing around. They didn't seem to be in much of a hurry. Not taking it *too* seriously then, he thought. The ferry was waiting at the end of the jetty, half loaded with vehicles, nothing currently going on or coming off. Declan stopped at the far end of the queue, a little too suddenly and with a clunk. He realised he'd scraped a metal bollard at the side of the road. He decided to leave the Porsche here and make the rest of the way down to the ferry on foot.

The rain was coming down in earnest now, no light summer shower. As Declan reached the embarkation point of the ferry, he saw that the police had blocked it off with their own vehicles, a panda and an unmarked car. A man in a padded jacket who Declan took to be the marksman was standing by the two police officers. He was armed with a semi-automatic, the kind you might see them carrying outside

10 Downing Street. And there was another chap in a green waxed coat with a gun – that would be the vet, Declan thought. Why was he carrying a gun? Oh, a tranquillizer dart gun of course. That made perfect sense if there really was a wild animal on the loose. All this was running through his mind as he tried to push his way past and onto the ferry.

'Sorry, Sir, no one is allowed on deck. Go back to your vehicle and wait. This shouldn't take long,' said the younger of the two policemen.

'What's going on?'

'Just go back to your vehicle, Sir,' the officer repeated firmly.

Declan took a step backwards, but in the shadows between the rows of cars on the deck he saw a shape that might have been a large cat or might have been no more than a shadow slipping by, and without pausing to think, he took a leap onto the deck of the ferry, pushing the young policeman to the ground.

*

Declan landed awkwardly, steadied himself and looked around – no sign of the cat. But behind him the policeman was shouting, and a small knot of men came running up to follow him onto the ferry. Declan looked around for somewhere to disappear, but it wasn't him they were pursuing.. They'd seen something else. He shrank into the space between a white van bearing the faded name *Barycz Building & Plumbing* and a people carrier.

'This thing would bring down an elephant,' the vet in the

green waxed jacket was saying, as he walked by Declan's hiding place.

'Wouldn't have thought there was much call for bringing down an elephant in Woolwich,' said the police marksman, carrying his own far superior weapon that looked like it could do serious damage to an elephant and more or less obliterate a smaller animal. 'Supposed to be a big cat, isn't it?'

'Strictly speaking the big cats are the lion, tiger, jaguar, leopard and snow leopard. It won't be one of them. There are thirty or more smaller cats – such as the puma, the lynx, the Scottish wild cat – and it won't be any of *them* either. It'll be somebody's old moggy, one of those upmarket breeds – a Bengal, Maine Coon, or something of that ilk.'

'Waste of our time then.'

'Unless it's something that's been smuggled in – maybe something with rabies?'

*

Declan waited until they had gone past, then came out from between the vehicles. The back doors of the white van were wide open, revealing all the usual junk of a builder's trade, and Declan took a moment to catch his breath and sit on the tail of the van out of the rain.

There was a lurch and a movement beneath him and he realised that the ferry was moving out into the river. Someone must have decided that this was the best way to isolate the creature? He rested a hand on the floor of the van beside him and it felt wet, but when he looked it wasn't rain – it was blood. He could hear people approaching, and shrank back into the van, pulling one of the doors closed before they passed by.

'Damn silly wild goose chase,' came the voice of a policeman, walking between the row of cars on the deck.

'I definitely saw something moving over there,' came a second younger voice, sounding unsure, 'didn't you?'

Declan felt the ferry stop moving beneath him and wondered if they were going to give up the chase after all. After a few moments, he climbed out of the back of the van to resume his own search, walking between the vehicles each with tightly closed windows and doors and drivers shut inside, some annoyed, some bored with waiting. No one looked particularly scared as they scrolled through their phones. He didn't have far to go, before he found what he was looking for.

Flattened against the side of a lorry, white faced and terrified, was a short, chunky man. There were a deep wounds across his face, and along his chest a long gash, visible through a ripped shirt. The man's eyes were fixed on the bonnet of a car opposite, where some kind of animal crouched getting soaked in the rain and snarling. Ears flattened. This was not the puma from that night in the little church on Blackheath – this was a badly drawn cat, smaller than Declan remembered, slightly lopsided, with longer ears and a cruel row of bared teeth. The creature looked like it had been thrown together in a hurry by the shaky hand of some inebriated minor deity. Puma, lynx or whatever it was, it might be Cass, or her *tulpa* creation. Or it might be nothing of the kind. It occurred to him that he would look like a complete idiot if it did turn out to be someone's escaped pet moggie after all. There was no way of knowing for sure, but he had to take a chance. He had to reach out to her before it killed or was killed.

'Cass!' he shouted, and the cat turned for second to hiss and spit at him, breaking its gaze from the terrified man by the lorry.

At that point things began to move fast and become muddled. The chunky little man tried to make a run for it, the cat leaped off the car bonnet after him, the marksman, the two police officers and the vet heard the commotion and doubled back quickly. Declan tried calling a warning them not to hurt the animal. But that didn't go down well.

'Get back here! Are you mad?' yelled the older policeman.

'No! The animal's not dangerous! Please don't frighten her.'

'Get down on the floor *now*,' the marksman rapped out, raising his semi-automatic. As did the vet with his tranquilliser gun that could bring down an elephant, whilst the younger PC radioed for back up, ambulances, and the RSPCA. Or maybe Declan imagined that bit.

As the chunky little man ran towards the railings, Declan and the cat followed, while the marksman tried to take aim through the lashing rain.

'Get out of the way!' bawled the marksman.

'No! You can't shoot her.' Declan shouted back at him.

'But I can,' came the vet's voice. 'It's some kind of hybrid, I reckon.'

Ducking and running, the chunky little man in the torn and bloody shirt made a sudden dive for the side of the ferry, but the wild cat leapt at him, knocking him over the side, falling with him. Declan was right behind them. As he reached the railings, something hit and stung his arm, and he found himself tumbling overboard in a tangle of limbs that might have been human or cat or both.

The water was so cold, and he was sinking. His left arm hurt, and Declan wondered of he'd been shot – his hand found something stuck in his upper arm – not a bullet then – something else – something he needed to pull out quickly before – but his head was becoming muzzy, he couldn't breathe, and there were arms coming towards him through the water – only they weren't arms but forelimbs with paws with sharp claws ...

*

She was cold and wet, sinking in deep grey water where she had no business to be, and absolutely no idea how she had got here. Or even who she was. She opened her eyes underwater and took a moment to adjust. There was a face, a body, someone familiar, someone drowning in front of her. Someone dangerous, someone who had once hurt her – or was that someone else? It was all muddled up in her head, but the shock of hitting the water had begun to clear away the fog. And all at once the only thing she *did* know for sure was that this was Declan, and that she had to save him.

She paddled furiously with her strong hind limbs, arms stretching out – but when she looked down at herself, she could see paws with sharp claws reaching out for him. *That was all wrong… still…* Her feline claws dug into his shoulder, sharp fangs into his neck in a fierce love bite, and began pulling him upwards through the water. And by the time they broke through the surface, she was holding him in her naked human arms.

'Come on, Declan,' she shouted at him, 'Don't go all Titanic on me now! Keep swimming! Use all your anger and passion, whatever it was, to keep you alive – think of all those icy cold Norwegian fjords you swam in! Are you *listening* to me?'

He opened his eyes and looked at her woozily. 'Cass, I knew you'd come back to me…' And then someone threw out a lifebelt for them, and not before time, thought Cass.

*

She was sitting on the side of the ferry, back at the slipway, as they pulled a body out of the river. She recognised him at once. He was dead, but not by her hand – or claws – he had drowned in the cold, unforgiving water.

'That's the man who attacked me,' she said. 'I know him, it's Mr Barycz.' She was wrapped in a vet's green wax coat, having no clothes of her own.

'He tied you up in the back of the van, and you got loose on the ferry?' asked the older policeman.

'Yes, I already told you all that. Now I want to go in the ambulance with Dr O'Neil, please.' The paramedics were carrying Declan into the ambulance as she watched, turning her face away from the police and other curious eyes.

'Well, you can give us your statement later.' The officer looked confused, as well he might, but she wasn't going to enlighten him. She was not sure she could enlighten him just now. There were some questions best left unanswered until you could come up with some really good lies. Ask any politician.

Chapter 27

Straight Street

Sometimes as you wake up there is a moment or two when you are not absolutely sure which was the dream and which is the reality of everyday life. Were you only a few moments ago in deep conversation with someone long dead, like Albert Einstein? Sitting in Patisserie Valerie eating Apfelstrudel with the distinguished scientist? Or climbing a misty Scottish mountain in the snow wearing nothing but your Speedos and flip flops? Or were you swimming in the icy waters of a deep river that seemed so cold, so real? Or were you dreaming of lying in a strange bed, with that unmistakable hospital smell around you?

When Declan opened his eyes the first thing he saw was Cass curled up on a chair beside his bed, with a hospital blanket draped around her legs.

'Oh, you decided to wake up. You took your time,' she said.

'Have you been sleeping here?' he asked.

'They checked me out and let me stay here to keep an eye on you. You've been out of it for two days. That's what happens when you get yourself shot by a vet with a tranquillizer dart, I guess.'

'I'll try not to do it again,' he said. 'Can I have a drink?'

'Of course. You're not nil by mouth.' She handed him a glass of water from the bedside locker. He drank it slowly, trying to recall the events that had led him here, so far as he could. Then he rang for the nurse to take him to the loo. He really needed the loo, and explanations could wait.

He found he could walk without much discomfort though his arm was still sore. He examined his face and upper body in a mirror on the bathroom wall. There were scratches on his shoulder and back that would take a while to fade. But all things considered he hadn't come out of it too badly – being shot at, attacked by a wild cat, half drowned and hauled out of the river. Now all he needed to know was what the hell had happened to cause this train of events. And for that Cass had to tell him whatever she remembered before the cat replaced her somewhere along the way.

*

'You opened the door to him?' Declan said in disbelief, 'Why? Was he delivering a red rose? Your sister has this theory about him being disguised as a delivery man. She posted something on some website, and it's gone viral – I bet Interflora are really pissed off.'

'No, Mr Barycz didn't have any red roses, Declan, he didn't need them when he came to my flat, I'd already given him my spare keys, remember? And he didn't have any roses when he came to *yours* either – he had one of those little cards – the ones you hand out to your private patients? Alison says they're like gold dust. People pass them on to their friends, sell them on eBay…'

'But I only give them a contact number,' he objected.

'This one had your address scribbled on the back. It was quite old and grubby, looked like he'd been carrying it around for a while. He was asking for your help.'

'Oh, Christ,' Declan groaned. 'Maybe I did give my home address to a couple of random patients when I first started out and had nowhere else to meet? Those phone calls I was getting – that must have been him too. I should have answered, perhaps I could have done something if he was asking for help.'

'*Might* have been him, not *must* have been him,' Cass said. 'You don't know that it *was* him. Anyway, Barycz was pretty surprised to find me there. But when he turned to leave, I saw the claw marks on the side of his face and neck, and I *knew*. I couldn't hide it, but I shouldn't have reacted. He might have walked away.'

'I doubt it. Once he guessed that you'd recognised him as your attacker, he had to get you out of the way.'

'He hit me so hard I nearly passed out, and then he pulled me down two flights of stairs – I tried to scream but he had his hand over my mouth. He dragged me into the underground car park and pushed me into the back of his van – then he must have hit me again and knocked me out this time. Because that's all I remember – until I came to in the water and saw you drowning in front of my eyes.' She shuddered and gripped his hand more tightly.

'Cass, can't you remember anything else? Nothing of the puma or whatever that thing was?'

She shook her head. 'Not really, I was subsumed into it, I suppose. All I can recall are feelings, sensations – fear, anger, power, a will to survive.'

'You must have changed places with it when you were locked in that van. Consciously or unconsciously you called it into being, then the swap happened. When your Mr Barycz opened the van doors, he got more than he bargained for. That would account for the blood in the back of his van – not your blood but his.'

Cass had been sitting quietly curled up in the most comfortable of the visitors' chairs, half wrapped in her blanket, but now she settled herself on the foot of Declan's bed and helped herself to some of the grapes from the bowl on top of his locker.

'What I really want to know is why – *how* – did I come back this time?' she said. 'All I remember is feeling drawn into the water – and then feeling very, very cold. And wet. I don't think cats like the water, do they?'

'I'd like to believe you came back because I needed you, and *you* didn't need the puma any more. That's one explanation, another is that the shock of hitting of the water did the trick – it reset your brain to default. In the Middle Ages there was a holy well in the little village of St Cleer in Cornwall, where people came from miles around for its healing properties. Apparently, the cold, pure waters of St Cleer were very effective in the treatment of the insane. They used to throw them down the well.'

'That's a bit harsh, isn't it, even for the Middle Ages?'

'No, they didn't *drown* them, they were fished out again after a brief cold-water treatment that seems to have worked like some kind of primitive ECT, if the stories are to be believed. Perhaps something similar happened to you when you went into the river?'

'Did it ever occur to you that maybe those poor souls learned to hide their craziness, so they didn't get thrown down that bloody well again?'

'I don't know. I'm beginning to think there are quite a lot of things I don't know anymore. But I believe in your case the combination of emotional and physical shock achieved something almost miraculous – it put you back together again.'

'And what about us?' said Cass.

'That's the one thing I *do* know,' he said. 'How can I put it? The people of Naples live beneath a volcano so powerful that if it blew tomorrow there'd be no chance of evacuating the city in time. It might happen tomorrow – or it might never happen in their lifetimes – they have to take a chance. I can live with that, if you can?'

'Are you saying I'm a *volcano* now? Thanks!'

'No, Cass, but you're a force of nature. Human nature, animal nature, like all the rest of us. And we have to muddle along, keeping our souls in balance as best we can, as Rabbi Schneu Zalman would say.'

Cass looked blank at the unfamiliar name. She stretched and pulled herself to her feet. 'I'm going to leave you for a while. I need to go back to yours and fetch you some clothes. Your Marge brought me a few things to wear from her own wardrobe. She's really nice, isn't she?' The navy tracksuit she was wearing was a little on the large side, but kindly meant and gratefully received along with a pair of nurse's shoes.

'How are you going to get into the flat?

'I've got your keys, silly, they were still in your pocket when they cut your clothes off you.' She opened the locker by his bed to reveal nothing but a box of tissues and a pair of shoes. 'The shoes have dried out. Everything else has gone.'

'What about money'

'If you had a wallet on you, it's at the bottom of the Thames. Pity. But Ted came by and gave me enough for taxis and phone calls, and whatever.'

'*Ted's* been here?'

'Oh yeah, and he'll be back at Visiting Hour now that you're awake.'

'Oh, shit!'

'Don't stress, it will be OK. Have some lunch, get a nap in before this afternoon. I'll be back later,' she said and kissed him on the forehead. 'Cheer up, here comes your consultant to check you over and I can see the tea trolley not far behind.'

Chapter 28

Visiting Hour

Lunch was not too bad, Cass had chosen the vegetarian lasagne option for him, followed by apple crumble and custard. You can't go far wrong with custard, Declan thought, so long as you bash out the lumps and avoid burning it in the pan. The tinned variety was the best bet in his opinion.

The consultant had been pleased with his progress and would allow him to go home tomorrow morning, so that was all good. He'd had a shower, managed to read a couple of newspapers from the little shop run by the WRVS and treated himself to a packet of extra strong peppermints from the small change Cass had left on his locker for him. He was feeling a bit more human. Now, despite having slept solidly for a couple of days, he was beginning to nod off again as the ward started to admit visitors.

He was about to pull the curtains around the bed when there was a bustle and a kerfuffle at the door, and a small deputation from the Sunshine Day Centre appeared. Big Malcolm was waving some flowers, a couple of the older ladies had brought fruit, and Davy slipped a large bar of chocolate out from under his denim jacket and slapped it onto the bedside locker.

'Oh, it's all right, Dr O'Neil,' said Patsy, perching herself on the foot of the bed, 'He paid for it at the little shop. He's a good boy.'

'It's wonderful to see you,' said Declan. 'But what about your afternoon sessions? Is there anyone covering for me while I'm stuck in here?'

'We're taking a break,' Malcolm informed him, 'just till you're on your feet. And we're not all going to be there when you do come back.'

'Why, what's happened?' asked Declan. Surely the funding cuts hadn't hit the Sunshine Day Centre this quickly? Was this going to be another battle to fight?

'I've got myself a job,' announced Malcolm proudly. 'It's at the dry cleaners where Maggie from the laundrette works now. They need someone to do the heavy lifting and she said I'd be perfect. Only two days a week to start with to see how I get on.'

'That's brilliant! But what about the rest of you?'

'Oh, we're still coming, aren't we?' said Patsy, nodding at the other older ladies. 'But our Davy's going back to school.'

'Yeah, I've got a place in a school for refusers like me, with small classes and special mentoring and everyfink,' said Davy.

'Davy, why is your face that bright pink colour? It looks quite painful,' said Declan.

'I fell asleep under my Mum's sun lamp the other day – well, you got to look good to get a girlfriend, ain't you? It's a bit sore now, but I'll have a good tan by tomorrow, you'll see.'

'Well that's wonderful news from Malcolm and Davy,' said Declan, looking beyond them for another face that was missing. But perhaps it was too soon.

'We won't stay any longer,' said Patsy, 'you need your rest.'

'We just came by to see that you were on the mend,' said Malcolm, as Patsy chivvied them towards the door.

Declan thanked them and waved goodbye, watching them stop to have a word with one of the nurses on their way out. The young woman looked familiar, but he couldn't quite place her till she came over to his bedside.

'Well, Dr O'Neil,' she said, 'you gave us a bit of a scare. It's my tea break, so I thought I'd pop up and see how you are.'

'Annie? Annie, I'm so pleased to see you. You're back at work already?' ECT could have a dramatic effect in lifting low mood, but he was concerned about the temptation to take on too much too soon. He didn't need to say anything, she knew what he was thinking.

'Look, I'm fine, I won't overdo it, I promise. They've let me go back on the ward part-time, then full-time in another month, all being good.'

'OK, that sounds do-able,' he said, 'I suppose that means you won't be coming back to the group either?'

'There'll always be others waiting to fill up the spaces – too many others,' said Annie. 'You concentrate on getting better. Funny me telling you that, isn't it?'

'It's what you do, Annie, you help people. But please don't

forget to look after yourself along the way.'

'I won't. Goodbye, Dr O'Neil,' she said, and hurried back to work. There was a different aura about her today from the sad eyed girl of the Sunshine Day Centre group sessions. A kind of sparkle. He hoped that she would find the secret of how to live, whatever it meant for her, and learn how to hold on to it this time.

As for Malcolm with his broad, smiling face, well, you could only hope that things would work out for him at the dry-cleaner's. Declan remembered the first time he had seen Malcolm lose it in a group session – something going on with one of the other patients had upset him, he felt it all too much, and he exploded. He tore off his glasses and snapped them between his fingers, but that wasn't nearly enough, so he picked up a chair and smashed it into pieces against a wall. He had to be restrained by two of the nurses before he calmed down. That gave an inkling of what was going on inside the big man. Declan could only hope nothing occurred to bring on an outburst like that in the outside world, or Malcolm could find himself back in prison alongside Joe who'd been arrested after screaming all night outside Woolwich Police Station. Declan made a mental note to check if Joe would be coming back to the Day Centre? Annie was quite right, there would always be plenty of others to fill up the spaces. Maybe this was the place where he was meant to be, trying to make a difference day by day, maybe so.

*

Cass reappeared towards the end of Visiting Hour, with a

holdall full of clothes, an electric razor and a comb. 'So you look a bit more presentable when I bust you out of here tomorrow,' she said, sitting on the visitor's chair. 'We could sneak down the Fire Escape.'

'It's OK, I'm being discharged. No need for dramatics. You can collect me around 10 a.m. tomorrow.'

'Good. I'll book a taxi, or maybe Ted can do the honours? I'll get you back to yours, then I really, really must go and see what kind of state my flat's in. I am going to be so angry if my laptop's been wrecked – my phone – my duvet. But I'm going to stay calm, rise above.'

'Cass?'

'What?'

'You do know it's OK to get angry every now and then?'

'Of course.'

'Remember when you first came to see me you said you needed help with anger management? And this whole *tulpa* thing, whatever it is, seems to be born of suppressed rage?'

'So I just need to keep it under control,' she nodded.

'Or maybe you need to change your attitude towards anger, rather than supressing it till it explodes like a bottle of pop you've been shaking too hard? Isn't it anger that gives us the energy to make choices for what we feel we need to do? The vital energy that propels us towards out goals?'

'Maybe, if you put it that way.' She sounded unsure.

'Channelling all that amazing anger and energy could become a positive thing, if you weren't so afraid of it?'

'I suppose so. I'll have to think about it.' She leaned

forward and kissed him on the cheek. Her hair smelled of thyme and mint, she must have washed it when she went back to the flat, he thought.

'Can you manage another visitor?' She pointed towards the door. It was Ted, not someone you could put off easily.

Declan nodded. 'You make your escape, I'll give him the official version – you were abducted by the bloke who attacked you, turns out to be the Deptford Wolf, you got free from his van on the ferry, and while all that business with the puma was going on you saw me accidentally get shot and fall in the river. That's when you dived in and rescued me. Is that it?'

'Close enough. Oh, and they're saying now it wasn't a puma at all, but a hybrid Savannah cat that got free from some private zoo a week ago – could be difficult to find. They're very elusive.'

*

Ted was on a tight schedule as usual, could only stay a little while, he was taking Alison and the girls off to look at some puppies this afternoon, he explained.

'Alison says the girls are old enough to be responsible, I've told her that's complete bullshit and she'll end up looking after any dogs we have, and she said *what else is new?*' He shrugged.

'What sort of dog?'

'I'm not sure. A Cockerpoo? A Labradoodle? One of those new breeds that won't shed fur on the upholstery. Anyway, soon find out when we get there. Alison's on her way back from her mother's now, they had to stay with her a couple more days – quite a funny story. Grandma went out the front door to look at the supermoon around 10 o'clock that night. She left the outside lights off, so she'd see it better, forgot how many steps there were down to the garden, fell down the lot, bumped into Allie's car on the driveway and landed in a heap. Then Allie went out and picked her up, with Grandma still insisting on toddling down the path to see the supermoon! But it was too cloudy. The whole thing's captured on their CCTV – the girls think it an absolute hoot. Oh, Grandma's all right – tough old bird, grazed her knees and bruised a shoulder. Didn't do any damage to the car,' he laughed. 'So, what about you? All's well that ends well, I guess? You should have told me what was going on, I would have come with you – or called the police.'

'Honestly, I had no idea, till I got down there,' said Declan. 'I got a text from Cass and knew I had to find her.' This was only marginally stretching the truth. There had been no text, just a wild hunch when he saw that TV News item on the screen.

'Don't worry, Cass gave me the Cliff Notes, you can fill me in later, when you're back on your feet.'

'I'm really sorry about your Porsche, Ted.'

'No problem. It's with Jarrod's, they specialise in respraying high-end vehicles for the export market. They'll get rid of the scratches.'

'Ted, do you know what kind of business it is they run down there?'

'Yes, very reliable, very cheap – and that's all I need to know. Now, about Blonde Pharmaceuticals –'

'Ted, I'm not interested in the drug trials.'

'That's OK, they've cancelled the drug trials. Gene therapy is the next big thing – now if we can cut ourselves a bit of the action – well!'

'*Cut ourselves a bit of the action?*' Declan laughed.

'It's the future, Dec, think about it. Sorry, I have to dash off now, Alison will have my guts for garters if I'm not home when they get back. They're all excited about going to see these Cockerpoo-doodle things.'

'That'll be expensive, won't it?'

'No, we're going to one of those Dog Rescue places full of poor old mutts wanting "forever homes". Won't cost me a thing – apart from the vet's fees for neutering and microchipping and inoculations, pet insurance, training classes, the grooming parlour, and all that dog food. No such thing as a free lunch, eh?' He grinned and made a gesture of resignation. 'Still, I suppose it will be good for the kids, keep us all healthy taking it for walks, whatever it turns out to be. Ciao!'

As Ted left, Declan could see Cass walking down the ward carrying two mugs of tea. She paused for a moment to exchange a couple of words with Ted, before he hurried off to his puppy appointment with Alison and the kids. Declan was relieved that he hadn't needed to do any explaining. As usual he had left Ted to do most of the talking. It worked better that way, he found.

Cass was coming back, Declan thought, with a sense of contentment. But then a thought struck him: what if it happened all over again? What if they couldn't bring the *tulpa* under control next time? And then he wondered what it would be like to have the power to breathe life into your own thoughts? Could anyone do it, or was it a rare talent, a random mutation, a one in a million thing that she possessed? Could he do it? Would he even want to try?

He knew he had promised that he'd be there for her come what may. Like living under a volcano – a bit of a cliché! But as a psychiatrist he knew that people's lives were made up of as many broken promises as ones honoured – usually far more broken than kept. Best to take things one day at a time, even if that led to an uncertain future. Maybe Cass was his future, his 'forever home', maybe not.

He settled down more comfortably against his pillows and closed his eyes. He knew she'd be there when he opened them again, and that was enough for now. Forever would just have to take care of itself.

Chapter 29

Off the Spine

Cass was walking down the hill towards the nearest local shops for a pint of milk and a cheap newspaper for her daily crossword fix when the call came. Not a familiar number but a familiar voice. He wanted to know how she was doing and if they could meet up for lunch?

'When? Today?'

'Yes, if you're free?'

'What for? I thought we'd said everything we had to say?'

'Cass, please, it's just lunch – in Hampstead? I need to see you before I leave. I'll meet you at the Tube around one?'

'You owe me more than a free lunch!' But already she was weakening, curiosity overcoming her better judgement. What did he mean 'before I leave'?

'Text me when you arrive. This is my new number. See you later!'

Damn it, the milk and the newspaper would have to wait – there was a bus pulling in at the nearest stop that would take her down to Blackheath station, and she could just catch it if she ran for it.

*

Cass had ten minutes or so in hand when she stepped out of

the Tube into the sunshine of Hampstead. She paused and looked around, it was always busier than she remembered in the days when she and Josh used to come up here in their own little bubble. Lunches in Hampstead were a bit of a treat – not something they could afford that often.

Over the other side of the Tube exit was a young man engrossed in his phone, like anyone else, except he wasn't just anyone. He was casually dressed in a blouson jacket that looked suspiciously like designer label, and well-fitting jeans. Tanned and slim, there was 'more of Apollo than Hercules' about him as Edgard Rice Burroughs had once described his ideal Tarzan, but Cass knew that hours of work in the gym with a personal trainer had honed that body to near perfection. She remembered the first time she'd seen him, in the bar at Uni, and he'd taken her breath away. She sighed and pinged a text at his phone. Josh turned and saw her, flicking his dark hair away from his eyes and waving.

'Cass! You came. I wasn't sure that you would,' he said.

'Yeah, well, here I am.'

'Would you like to go for a walk on the Heath? It's great weather.'

'No! You promised me lunch. I've trawled myself all the way across London on that promise, so now you can keep it.'

'Fair enough. The pub?'

Cass nodded. The pub meant their pub, the one they both liked, though they usually opted for the mac and cheese as the cheapest thing on the menu. Maybe today they could splash out a little?

Seated at a corner table with a large glass of red and a bowl of mac and cheese each (why change the habits of a lifetime?) Cass was wondering what had brought this on, this sudden desire to get together with the ex? Maybe Josh would suggest that they go on that TV programme? What was it called – *Eating with Your Ex? Sleeping with Your Ex?* She shuddered. She wouldn't put it past him if he thought it would boost his career. Though he seemed to be doing OK in that daytime police series – *Bishop & Co* – the one about the fish-out-of-water cockney DI relocated somewhere up North where he didn't speak the dialect but managed to solve crimes with the help of his local sidekick, played by Josh. He was always good at accents.

'Killed off,' he said, pausing between mouthfuls of pasta in a creamy cheese sauce with just a hint of nutmeg.

'What? You've been killed off?'

'Yes, the actor playing Bishop has baled – got a better job offer elsewhere, though that's confidential. Never name a TV series after the main character – honestly you think they'd have twigged that after that cult sci-fi thing? What was it called? *Blake's Seven?* Anyway, rather than just sticking with the original title and finding another DI with a new angle – I mean he could have been Welsh, or anything – they decided to cancel series three, and have written in a big dramatic ending for series two.'

'Don't tell me you get blown up?'

'Something like that – but Bishop goes back to his old job in London, all is forgiven. So my character is definitely toast, even if his has some future resurrection.'

'Sorry.'

'Actually, it was all for the best. Come on, let's go for a walk – how about Kenwood?'

Kenwood House had been a favourite weekend excursion when the weather was good, and once a magical evening of fireworks and music by the lake. Something to remember.

'You driving us up there?' she asked as they left the pub together.

'Ah, no, not exactly. The Skoda – well, the Skoda is now an ex Skoda. There was a little accident.'

'You totalled my Skoda!'

'Technically *my* Skoda,' he said, looking slightly shamefaced for a moment, eyes downcast. Then he smiled at her, and she couldn't be bothered to be angry with him. Oh, she *had* been angry with him for a long time – as angry as the Genie in that *Thief of Bagdad* film she so loved as a kid, the one where the boy releases the Genie from the bottle where it's been trapped for thousands of years plotting revenge, and it swears to kill him on the spot. So the boy tricks the Genie back into the bottle and only lets him out on the promise of good behaviour and the usual three wishes. Bottled up anger could be very dangerous – hadn't Declan said as much? – so you needed to release it very carefully.

'Come on, let's take a walk up to the Heath, that's not too far,' said Josh, taking her hand. And she didn't resist. On the way, broken only by a stop to buy a lemon Calippo and a mint Magnum from a roadside ice-cream van, Cass filled him

231

in with the sketchiest details of her own recent adventures in response to his queries. Fortunately Josh did not press her to reveal more than she was willing to share, and his concern seemed genuine. And there was still the issue of the Skoda – perhaps that was weighing on his mind. They walked the last few yards up to the Heath in silence, concentrating on their ices. It was a warm day and you don't want a mint Magnum melting chocolate down the front of your designer jacket, do you?

*

'So, I was driving through Hemel Hempstead on the Magic Roundabout –' said Josh.

'What were you doing there?'

'Blame Satnav. I'd had a day's filming up at Whipsnade Zoo and Satnav said this was the direct route home. As it turns out it wasn't. You remember that intermittent fault the Skoda had?'

Cass shuddered and nodded. The words Intermittent Fault are the ones you never want to hear from a car mechanic. It means they can't pin it down unless it actually happens on their forecourt.

'The Skoda died on me on one of those little mini roundabouts. So I got out for safety, as you would, stepped onto the kerb and started calling the AA when this fucking great artic comes round and totally misjudges the curve – slams into the Skoda and practically destroys it. All I managed to save was one of the wing mirrors that was sheared off in the impact. I thought I might give you it as a souvenir but thought better of it.'

'My God!'

'Yes, kind of a lucky escape. But I won't need the Skoda where I'm going.'

They paused for a few moments to look at the green space at the top of the hill, so familiar yet so different now. When they used to walk up here, they were together, discussing a future – a proper home, a dog, maybe even a baby? Things that never happened, though they did have a cat for a while. A big, black cat called Butch, remembered fondly, who went AWOL one day never to be seen again.

'Where's that then?'

'New Zealand. Five months filming a new American TV series – *Return of the Warrior Princess.*'

'Wow! You didn't tell me. Decent money?'

'Very decent money and a decent part. I'm some kind of demi-god wandering around playing a lute – or a lyre – or a flute – whatever it is I'll pick it up. You know me.'

Yes, she did know. Josh was one of those annoying people who could pick up any instrument and play it well enough to get a job in a tour of *Forbidden Planet* straight out of Uni, while she was still struggling to get work. It was only when she switched to production that things began to take off for her. By then Josh had decided 'musicals weren't his thing' and went for a year's course in drama at Bristol Old Vic Theatre School, supported by Cass, then reinvented himself as a straight actor. He owed her not just for the car, but for his career prospects.

'When do you go?'

'Next week. That's why I wanted to see you and say goodbye. I'm aiming to move to America after this series.'

'I see. All that networking's paid off then?'

'Huh! God knows. If this show doesn't get cancelled after one series, there's hope! Anyway, I wanted to tell you I put a payment into your bank this morning. For your share of the Skoda.'

'Oh, I wasn't expecting it.'

'Weren't expecting me to pay up anytime soon? Well I can, and I have. Check your account later and don't bother to thank me – it's probably nowhere near as much as I owe you.' He brushed her cheek with his hand and Cass did not draw away. 'For what it's worth I still love you to pieces – but you always knew it couldn't last forever? However hard we tried to make it work?'

Cass nodded and said he was probably right and that she had to get back home because she'd only gone out for a pint of milk and a paper. And they walked back to the Tube station where Josh kissed her goodbye like a brother, and she wished him good luck in New Zealand and don't forget to wear sunscreen because you know what you're like. And then she went down into the station, hoping it wouldn't be too busy, and that she wouldn't cry, because there was no reason to cry, was there?

*

Only one part of the underground was crowded, the stretch between Holborn and Bank. Cass had already checked her current account and put her phone away. She had not been expecting Josh to have transferred that much money. The new job must be paying really well! If that was going to be the last time she saw her beautiful ex-husband in the flesh, she thought, then it was just as well that her bottled up Genie anger had been diffused and that they had parted on civilised terms. Particularly as he'd just given her ten thousand pounds and the dear little ex Skoda was probably worth no more than three, tops.

As the door opened another flood of commuters squashed into the carriage, Cass found her backside pressed up uncomfortably close to a heavy man who was beginning to take advantage of chance proximity. Normally when wearing high heels her ploy was to rake the stiletto up the offender's shin. That usually stopped them dead. But today she was in trainers and wedged in so tightly that she could only turn her head to hiss like a scalded cat and utter a deep, throaty growl so effectively that a small child in his mother's arms burst into tears beside her. The heavy man got off at the next station and no one troubled her further.

Epilogue

Cass pulled up outside the house in her shiny new lipstick red Honda – an ex-forecourt model, a real snip. As she was walked up the path, Alison was opening the front door, on her way out with a buggy and Debbie.

'Hello stranger!' said Alison, bumping the buggy down the doorstep.

'What the hell is that thing?' said Cass, looking beyond her sister at the large – very large – dog sitting in the hall. It was black and furry, with tan and white markings and a big white cross on its chest. It had eyes like saucers, and a pink tongue. When it saw Cass approaching it lifted up one big paw in a kind of canine salute.

'That is not a *thing*, that is Sheba. A Bernese Mountain Dog from a broken home. Sad history. She's our new rescue dog.'

'My puppy,' said Debbie, hugging the said rescue dog around the neck and planting a kiss on her floppy ear. This puppy was bigger than Debbie.

'Come on,' said Alison, 'we're taking Sheba for a walk. You can push the buggy when Debs gets tired.'

'What does Ted say about the dog then? I thought he wasn't keen?' asked Cass.

'Well, actually she was *his* choice. We went to the animal

shelter to get something small – like a Cockerpoo – but when he saw Sheba, he went all peculiar. Said his Grandad had one just like her when he was a kid. Used to pull a little painted cart around the farm just for fun. She looked up at him with those big, gooey eyes and put a great big paw on his foot and that was it. A done deal.'

'She's very *large*, Alison… is she totally reliable? Are you sure she wasn't responsible for breaking up the last home?"

'I told you, she's a *Bernese* – very canny the Swiss: they breed a big strong dog that can pull a cart full of milk and cheeses around the mountain villages, but so docile and biddable it can be led by a young boy – so much cheaper than hiring a man with a pony and cart to deliver their goods. Any sign of aggression and the puppies were culled.'

'Why were the puppies cold, Mummy?' asked Debbie.

'Because it's very snowy up in the Swiss Alps, darling,' Alison answered without pausing. 'She's ever so gentle, and the kids adore her, they can do anything with her. But obviously I won't let them pull her around or dress her up. A dog is not a toy, is it Debs?'

A Swiss breed, eh? Trust Alison to do due diligence; she'd never fall instantly in love with a dog and take it home just because it was big and beautiful with sad, soulful eyes.

They took the road to the Village at a slow pace, with time for a stop at a café and a catch up. They sat at the pavement tables with Sheba obediently lying by their side, and Debbie enjoying a strawberry ice cream that occasionally dribbled blobs onto the dog's head beneath her.

'My flat's fixed up really well, thanks to the insurance,' said Cass. 'It's wonderful to have my own space again.'

'Oh, I thought you were with Declan now?' There was a very slight edge to Alison's voice. Cass had noticed a certain frostiness in her sister's demeanour of late, as Jane Austen might have put it in a much better novel.

'We are together, but we don't have to *live* together, do we? Not just yet anyway. There's no hurry, is there?'

'Oh, I see.'

'What do you mean? *Oh, I see?* Spit it out!'

'I just mean I hope you're not going to hurt him.'

'What? That's rich coming from you the one who broke his heart and went off with his best friend. Classic!'

'Ancient history. And I hope you understand that Declan and Ted are mates, and whatever you may feel about Ted, they've always been close. Back at Uni the three of us were never apart – I soon realised I was never going to break up that bromance. Then when Ted and I got together, it did get awkward for a while, but it sorted itself out.'

'Allie, I'm not out to break up any "bromance". But I thought *you* might be jealous, just a wee bit jealous?'

'No!' Alison shook her head. 'I want Declan to be happy – and I want *you* to be happy. So maybe you're right to take it one step at a time.' She took a napkin and wiped some of the ice cream off Sheba's head before it rolled down into the dog's mouth. Then she fed her a sneaky biscuit from a pocket full of dog treats. Sheba's furry black tail with its snow white tip beat a happy rhythm against Alison's leg.

'You never actually told me why you broke up with Declan and started seeing Ted back then?' said Cass, over her coffee.

'Oh, it was all such a long time ago,' said Alison with a shrug of the shoulders.

'Come on, there must have been a reason?'

'Something about Dexy unsettled me, there was always something a touch feral about him – that wild swimming thing and the way he loved to take chances, like that night when I locked myself out of the flat.'

'Go on, what did he do wrong?'

'He was drunk – we'd been at a party, we'd all been drinking – but he insisted on climbing up the side of that building and letting himself in through the window. I begged him not to, but he wouldn't listen to me, up he went, nearly fell a couple of times. He could have broken his neck. I never felt safe with him, I suppose. He enjoyed taking risks too much for my liking.'

'How strange, that's exactly why I feel safe with Declan, I know he'll take crazy risks for me. But you always felt safe with Ted?'

'Oh, yes, Ted would never take risks – he might damage his paintwork. Ted would have called out a twenty-four-hour locksmith and haggled down the price.'

Cass burst out laughing and Alison grinned back. After all they were sisters, they were different, they were the same.

END

Playlist

Quentin Tarantino and I have one thing in common – he likes to write to a soundtrack in his mind, creating a scene around a song. Same thing with me – but less violent. So here are the songs you'll find peppered throughout this novel, if only in my mind.

Total eclipse of the heart – Bonnie Tyler
Rasputin – Bony M   *I feel love – Donna Summer*
These are the disco tracks that give you a pounding headache at the end of a party that went on far too long and did not live up to the promise of a good time. We've all been there.

Storm Warning – Bonnie Raitt
Sad and poignant, about love going wrong. Bonnie Rait, by the way, is the daughter of John Raitt, star of *The Pyjama Game* one of Cass's favourite old musicals.

Come on Eileen – Dexy's Midnight Runners
Denim and slightly dubious lyrics, but a real ear worm.

Where or When – by Rogers & Hart
A strange, haunting melody about déjà vu, sung by many performers over the years, from Frank Sinatra to Harry Connick Jr. Originally from the 1937 musical *Babes in Arms*.

*You took the Words Right Out of My mouth (Hot Summer Night) –
Meatloaf. From the* Bat out of Hell *album by Jim Steinman*
I first heard this sitting in a small café in Chester after going
to a friend's wedding in Wales. The whole café fell quiet to
listen to the spoken intro and when the music rolled in with
Meatloaf's amazing voice I was hooked forever. Jim Steinman
has a way with stretching his metaphors like no other
songwriter I know.

Come back to me – sung by Yves Montand
This is from the musical *On a Clear Day You Can See Forever* by
Alan Jay Lerner & Burton Lane. If you watch the original
trailer as Declan did, you can see Yves Montand, as
psychiatrist Marc Chabot, belting out this song from the roof
of the Pan Am building. Why there? You might well ask. But
it has been listed as one of the top 100 musicals of all time.

Gentrification – Ry Cooder – The Prodigal Son *album*
This one just makes me laugh!

Supermoon – Laura Veirs & Necko Case
This is from the sublime *Case/Lang/Veirs* album (2016) that
my daughter gave me. You may have heard this track on a TV
programme about our near neighbour, the moon.

*There's a man in your closet duet – The Marriage of Figaro – Mozart
Hotel California – The Eagles*

I suggest you listen and compare these two and see what you think for yourselves.

'Mir ist die Ehre' – Presentation of the Rose – Der Rosenkavalier – Strauss

I was working as a dresser at Covent Garden when the Spanish seamstresses, Conchita and Maria, dragged me down to watch the Presentation of the Rose at a dress rehearsal. 'You must see this, it is magical,' said Conchita, and she was right.

You're so Vain – Carly Simon

The first time you hear her clever lyrics is always the best. Then you start wondering: who is it about – Warren Beatty? Mick Jagger? It could have been written for Josh Green, now doing so well for himself over in the States. He's up for a part in that new thing about the English doctor in Seattle who finds a cure for something embarrassing with a long name. I think it's a comedy.

Pink Moon – Nick Drake

You've probably heard this one on a TV commercial, but you'll hear the influence of Nick Drake's music coming through many later singer-songwriters. He died too young.

Straight Street – Ry Cooder - The Prodigal Son *album*

This is about the possibility of change and redemption and choosing happiness if you want it. By the end of this story I hope all my characters are on their way to *Straight Street,* even Ted. This is the song I want played at my funeral come the day. Or possibly:

Pray for You – Jaron and The Long Road to Love, the debut single from Jaron Lowenstein.

This is all about anger and how to channel it creatively! Cass would love this one.

Where do ideas come from? Generally I'd say they are drawn together from different aspects of your own life. The idea for this novel was knocking around for a very long time – I'd tried it out in various formats – a screenplay? A TV sitcom about two sisters? Maybe a novel one day in the future? But the quickest way to get the idea down on paper seemed to be as a short story, and I've only just found it again at the bottom of a box file of paperwork going back to the 1990s. In this very early version Cassandra is a jaded, older career girl and Alison is her 'baby sister'.

So here it is:

Never Cry Wolf

There must have been a particular day when Desiderata came down from Alison's kitchen bulletin board and the recipe for Playdough went up, but Cassandra couldn't for the life of her remember when. Alison was sitting opposite her at the table, twisting a buff envelope between her fingers.

'And they want me to pay up £587.80 in voluntary contributions by the 4th of April,' she repeated gloomily.

'If you haven't got it, that's it,' said Cass bluntly. She felt too tired for all this agonising.

'It's a straight choice between my old age pension and a set of ready-made stretch covers for the lounge suite,' Alison sighed.

'No contest!'

'Exactly, with Nigel, three kids, two cats and a dog climbing over the furniture, what choice do I have? It's all right for you, Cass, you've got your career, private pension plan, your own place –'

'Divorce costs, negative equity and a flat like a bomb site – but let's look on the bright side: we could both be dead before you pick up your pension.'

'I told you not to get cowboy builders,' said Alison.

'Catford cowboys come cheap – professional interior designers don't,' snapped Cass. She had been up since two in the morning away filming in darkest Pirbright and was in no mood to be criticised by her baby sister. Why should Alison worry about her DWP pension? Nigel and the company scheme would provide – unless, of course, their marriage crumbled too. But somehow Cass couldn't see Nigel running off with the Best Boy from *Eastenders* the way her Dermot had. No, Allie had nothing to worry about, sitting here in her beautiful Smallbone kitchen, all sunshine, fresh coffee aroma and daffodils.

'We were expecting you yesterday,' said Alison. 'I was worried when you didn't turn up.'

'Over-run. Why worry? I'm not your responsibility I'm a fully paid-up adult, almost geriatric,' Cass added with a tinge of bitterness. Just lately she found she didn't much like working for directors younger than herself.

Alison pushed the local paper across the table. *DEPTFORD WOLFMAN CLAIMS NEW VICTIM* and *FULL MOON WEREWOLF HORROR* ran the headlines. 'You can't be too careful,' she said.

'I don't live in Deptford,' Cass objected.

'Greenwich is near enough.'

'Just 'cos you live in Blackheath! Why do they call him the Deptford Wolf?'

'I suppose they think it sounds macho. I'd call him the Deptford Ferret, the Welling Weasel, the Plumstead Stoat – they're always weaselly little characters when they get caught.'

'Not necessarily – might be built like Mike Tyson.'

'Not this one. One of his victims got a good look at him, pulled off his balaclava before –'

'No need to go into prurient details.'

'She was one of the lucky ones – she got away.'

'I don't want to know.' Cass drained her coffee and put the mug down on the newspaper.

'You're probably in no more danger down there than we are up here,' Alison conceded. 'Anyway, most rapes and murders are by friends or colleagues, aren't they? It's when that hunky new neighbour from the flat upstairs comes down to borrow a jar of coffee that you want to slip the chain on the door.'

'Alison, you have an overactive imagination. I hardly think poor old Miss Meek is likely to come tripping back from the Twilight Zone for a jar of Gold Blend.' Cass shuddered as someone walked over her grave. 'I wish I hadn't said that…'

'Now who has an overactive imagination?' said Alison. 'You should think yourself lucky she popped off when she did – neighbours can be a pain. Her Next Door has been round again: apparently a rat has been seen at the bottom of the gardens. So now we're calling in the Environmental Health Officer. We'll have rat poison all over the place and the guinea pigs will eat it – Debbie might eat it – she ate a slug last week, well, I think she did, I found *half* a slug in her grubby little paw. Do you think she ate the other half? Cass?'

Cass was leaning back in her chair, eyes closed. 'No I'm listening – it's like the tinkling of a distant waterfall, all your little domestic problems. It puts my life into a whole new perspective.'

'Charming!'

'Sorry, it's just that I've been up since before dawn, standing around in a freezing graveyard with a bunch of zombies for a film crew looking more convincing than the extras playing zombies, and I'm only just beginning to unwind... Got anything to eat?' Cass realised that she was not just tired but starving. Somehow, she hadn't been able to face another greasy fry-up from the back of the caterer's wagon this morning.

'I'll put Debbie down for her nap and make you a sandwich. Then you can have a good old whinge about *your* life, and I'll tell you why mine's worse.' Alison gathered up the toddler who had been playing beneath the table and disappeared for a few moments.

Cass closed her eyes again and felt herself drifting off to a place somewhere between sleeping and waking, heard the sound of birdsong in the garden outside fade to nothingness, becoming aware of a deeper rhythmic pulse pounding through her head. But not her own pulse. Something else. Something wild. This shouldn't be happening! She shook herself awake.

Alison was back at the kitchen table making sandwiches, her sandy hair and freckled face reassuringly familiar. 'I've been stuck at home now for eight years,' she moaned. 'It feels like my brain's turned to boiled cabbage. Some days I don't even have the courage to poke my head outside the front door.'

'What are you afraid of?' Cass laughed. 'I don't understand?'

'Of course you don't, you've always done exactly what you wanted – good luck to you! I'm stuck here washing and cleaning and picking up after everyone, and every now and then I get the feeling I'm completely invisible.'

'It was your choice to have kids.'

'That's what Nigel says, as if he had nothing to do with it!'

'You always said you wanted three.'

'But not all at once! First the twins, then Debbie – and that was the dentist's fault.'

'*What?*' The sandwich hovered by Cass's mouth.

'Didn't I tell you? Remember when I had all that trouble with an abscess on my wisdom tooth? And he put me on antibiotics, and I asked him if it would be OK to take them because I was on the pill, and he said it was – well, it *wasn't.*'

'I didn't know that.' Cass frowned and took note.

'Neither did my dentist!' said Alison. Cass couldn't help laughing despite herself, and eventually so did Alison.

*

The sandwiches were all gone and Cass was helping Alison with the washing up. 'Allie, if I tell you something, you won't think I'm crazy?' she began.

'That depends.'

'It *is* crazy – but it did happen,' said Cass, 'one night at the unit hotel. I was trying to get some sleep – you know what these cheap hotel rooms are like: light coming in through the blinds, you can't get away from the noise?'

'All part of your glamorous lifestyle.'

'Production Assistant is hardly glamorous. Sheer hard slog – no life for a girl! So, I'm trying to get some rest but there's a party going on around the pool just outside my window. The music was thumping through my head. I couldn't stand it anymore.'

'So what did you do?'

'Put a stop to it,' said Cass grimly. 'I'd been reading this book by Dion Fortune – *Psychic Self-Defense* – all about magic. Ever hear of a *tulpa*?'

Alison shook her head and went on drying up.

'It's a thought-form, a creature of the imagination. An ancient Tibetan thingy.'

'I see.'

'No, you don't – but I was very tired, half asleep... I dreamed one up, right there in my hotel room. A wolf *tulpa*.' Cassandra felt once again the soft thrill of fur beneath her fingertips as she reached down from her bed and touched the wolf for the first time. Warm and *alive*, strong and sinewy. She could hear once again its harsh breathing and the gentle growl as she scratched behind its ears. The wolf liked that. She could smell the strange, fresh, tangy scent of distant tundra that the wolf brought with it and the touch of an icy wind sweeping through pine trees of faraway lands.

'You what?' said Alison.

'I dreamed the damn thing up and set it on the louts outside my window. Soon got rid of them.' Cass paused and licked her lips. Her mouth felt dry.

'So what's the problem?' said Alison, putting away the crockery.

'*I can't get rid of the wolf.* It comes back. Of its own accord. I keep on seeing it everywhere, anywhere…'

'Look, just after the twins were born, I'd been up most of the night, when I finally got to bed – with *both* of them in between me and Nigel – you know what happened?' said Alison. 'A hostile spacecraft landed on the back lawn and zapped us with a Martian Death Ray. I couldn't move, couldn't even scream, I was terrified. Thought they'd killed Nigel and the girls – it was awful! Next morning I had to go to the Well Baby Clinic and I just casually asked my GP about the Martian Death Ray thing, and he said it was a hypnogogic hallucination, a kind of waking dream you can get from lack of sleep.'

'Are you saying it's all in my mind?'

'Maybe you just need a good night's sleep?'

'Don't be patronising,' Cass sulked.

'*Me* patronising? That's rich! Don't you ever listen to yourself?'

'Oh Allie!' Cass felt a lecture coming on.

'You're forever sneering at me – you always find Brownies and NCT coffee mornings and Face Painting at the School Summer Fete so terribly amusing, don't you? Well, let me tell you, in this past month I've had three trips to Casualty with the kids, delivered thirteen Great Dane puppies for Mrs O'Hanlon when the vet didn't turn up, and saved Freya's life when she chocked on a 5p coin by doing this –' Alison grabbed Cassandra round the waist from behind and executed the Heimlich manoeuvre, a sharp inward and upward thrust that left Cass gasping. 'Only more gently with a child,' Alison admitted. 'These may not be great achievements in your scheme of things, but I'd like to see you cope with a kid turning blue in the face, or a seven stone Great Dane bitch in labour.'

'OK, you've made your point.' Cass staggered over to the kitchen table and sat down again. But Alison wasn't finished.

'And what have you been doing? Making glossy TV commercials that patronise women like me, implying that we spend our whole lives polishing our Agas and reading *Good Housekeeping* behind lacy white curtains.'

'You haven't got an Aga,' Cass protested.

'Don't quibble. Don't you forget, sister mine, I knew you back when you were plain old Carol Green – it was 'our Carol this' and 'our Carol that' from our proud Mum, until you came back after one term at university with scarlet hair and a brand-new name. After that we didn't hear so much about 'our Carol' unless it was spoken in whispers.'

'Pax! Fainites! Mea culpa,' begged Cass laughing. Alison's accusations had hit home, however. For half that year she'd been working on a series of lucrative commercials, amongst them was one promoting a new spritzer composed of soda water and elderflowers. Served icy cold on the rocks it was wonderfully refreshing but smelled like cat's pee. The brief had been to romanticise the product in a Joanna Trollopesque Aga-Saga setting: a sun dappled country kitchen with views across a village green, cricketers at the slips, a couple of pet Muscovy ducks wadding in through an open door, an attractive young couple sipping spritzers at an antique pine table. And cricket on the green was clearly not the only thing on their mind.

The Muscovy ducks were an inspired touch. Unfortunately one of the damn things went missing on the last day of the shoot, rumour had it into the back of a van belonging to one of the Grips, and from thence into his freezer. There was hell to pay with the Animal Wrangler.

'Pax,' agreed Alison, flopping down into a chair. 'Now what are you going to do?'

'About what?'

'Your wolf, stupid!'

'Thought you didn't believe in it?'

'Let's suppose, for argument's sake that it does exist.'

'Well, I've figured out one thing – it only appears when I'm angry, or afraid.'

'You always did have a nasty temper.'

'That's not very helpful.'

'But true. Don't you see? Fear and anger? The old fight or flight response? Get your adrenalin flowing and Wolfie comes running. You're *feeding* it with your anger.'

'No,' said Cass slowly, 'it *is* my anger.'

'Displaced anger,' Alison nodded. 'Oh, Cass, why is losing

your temper so unacceptable? Men do it all the time – why is it when we do it, it's like losing your knickers in public?'

'I can't afford to get angry. I have to be nice to people – actors, directors, producers – even if they are a bunch of dickheads.'

'Don't you think it's the same for me? I know people take of advantage of me – face painting, cake baking, school runs – and I bet Mrs O'Hanlon didn't even phone for the vet.'

'So you have the Martian Death Ray and I have Wolfie because we're both too damn nice?'

'Time I picked up the kids from school,' said Alison. 'Why don't you take a nap? Have the guest room, same as always.'

'Thanks. You're an angel.'

'I know.'

*

Cass lay down on the bed, sinking deep into the fluffy duvet with delight. She heard Debbie and Alison go out of the front door, walk to the car, and drive off. The sounds of outdoors began to fade as she listened to the sounds of the house. A quiet house in a nice, safe road. The slow clock ticking, cat purring at the foot of the bed, washing machine humming away downstairs. Was that the dog scrabbling at the back door to be let into the kitchen? The door creaking open… Alison must have forgotten to lock it, how careless! (But Blackheath is a long way from Deptford.) The sounds of soft, padding steps coming up the stairs and a nervous, rasping sound like a man struggling to control his own breathing…

A tiny jolt of adrenalin shot through Cassandra's body. To

her sleepy brain came the memory of that strange, fresh, tangy scent of distant tundra that the wolf always brought with it. And to her ears the faint pulse of a heart beating faster than her own.

A door handle clicked ever so slightly, and a cat jumped off the bed to hide beneath it. There was a soft growl that might have come from her own throat – or from something much wilder. But if anyone disturbed her now, she was going to get very, *very* angry.

END

Bibliography

Little Red – Amy Lane, Dreamcatcher 28, 2014, Stairwell Books, www.stairwellbooks.co.uk

Antigonish (I met a man who wasn't there) – William Hughes Mearns, 1899

Psychic Self-Defense – Dion Fortune, © 1930, 1997 Society for the Inner Light. First published 2001, Red Wheel/Weiser, LLC. Weiser Books, Boston, MA/York, ME

The Beast Within – Man, Myths and Werewolves – Adam Douglas 1992, Orion

Myths of the Norsemen – Roger Lancelyn Green 1971, A Puffin Original, Penguin Books

Seeking Whom He May Devour – Fred Vargas, translated from French by David Bellos,
The Harvill Press, London 2004, Random House, 20 Vauxhall Bridge Rd, SW1V 2SA

Mystery Big Cats of Dorset – Chris Moiser, 2007, Inspiring Places Publishing, 2 Down Lodge Close, Alderholt, Fordingbridge, Hampshire SP6 3JA

Magazine Articles

Lycanthropy, mythology and medicine – Hamdy F. Moselby, MB, Bch, MSc, Registrar, and Fiona MacMillan, MRCPsych, MD, Senior Lecturer in Psychiatry, University of Birmingham Honorary Consultant, All Saints Hospital, Lodge Road, Birmingham, B18 SSD, England. Correspondence, Published in the *Irish Journal of Psychological Medicine* 1994 December; ll (4):168 – 70

The Unexplained – Mysteries of Mind Space and Time – Volume 8, Issue 85 (1982) published weekly by Orbis Publishing Ltd., Orbis House, 20/22 Bedfordbury, London WC2N 4BT (OOP)

Tulpas The Word Made Flesh – Francis King

Beast of Gevaudan – Cornering the Beast – Gregory Pons

About the Author

Linda studied Drama/English at Hull University. Working as a dresser at the National Theatre and the Royal Opera House financed a postgraduate course in theatre design at Croydon Art College. She went on to work in theatre and TV costume design, then began writing following a NSCTP scriptwriting course at the National Film & Television School. She has taught Creative Writing for the Open University and writes scenarios for murder mystery parties. She's currently working on a practical handbook for running your own creative writing group.

Printed in Great Britain
by Amazon